TO SWALLOW A TOAD

A NOVEL BY

Peter Weston Wood

DONALD I. FINE, INC.
NEW YORK

Library of Congress Catalogue Card Number: 86-46398
ISBN: 1-55611-019-7
Manufactured in the United States of America
10 9 8 7 6 5 4 3 2 1.

Library of Congress Cataloging-in-Publication Data

Wood, Peter Weston.
To swallow a toad.

I. Title.
PS3573.05955T6 1987   813'54   86-46398
ISBN 1-55611-019-7 (alk. paper)

To Nathalie Alderman Pierce
and
Guy Wood.
With Love.

Nor law, nor duty bade me to fight,
Nor public men, nor cheering crowds,
A lonely impulse of delight
Drove me to this tumult in the clouds . . .

W. B. YEATS

ONE

THE FIRST FIGHT

No Brain, No Pain

This was it. This was the beginning. I sat quietly in the back seat, wallowing in my fear, yet ignoring it at the same time.

My trainer, Tom Brandy, drove. He was an angry old pug with facial scars like erosions and little tufts of gray hair that sprouted from each ear.

I didn't notice the filthy streets of Manhattan. I didn't smell the New York stench. I didn't hear the car radio. I was clamped shut, like a fist, steeped in my own theory. My theory was how I was going to break my opponent's face.

Violence squirmed inside my brain. Don't ask me why, or how. I don't know. But that's why I was sitting there in Tom's white Impala, wearing my hoody black hat and chewing a toothpick.

When violence squirms inside a guy's head, there's about three things he can do. He can do drugs, like my older brother; he can become mentally ill; or he can enter the Golden Gloves. I entered the Gloves.

As we drove closer to St. Jude's High School, where my first fight was, I remember thinking, I'll meet any hoodlum, wise-ass or tough guy in New York City, because whoever gets into the ring with me tonight had better have as much hate, anger, fear and violence as I do. Otherwise, I'll make his face dirt.

I guess I'd better introduce myself. I'm eighteen, a middleweight, and I've got the best left hook in this whole damn tournament. That's all you got to know.

Bobby Kemmelman, the other fighter in the car—another middleweight—sat next to me. We were both shooting for the same thing—the Middleweight Championship of New York City. However, I secretly knew that Bobby wasn't good enough to win. Gut level, he probably knew, too. And Sal Santora, Bobby's trainer, who sat up front with Tom, probably would have agreed.

But I liked Bobby. He trained hard. But not hard enough to lose the soft flab around his shoulders, stomach and whole body. He claimed that he was burly, but really he was just fat.

And he was ugly. It was his skin. Acne. His face was the color and texture of pizza. I always thought his face was the reason he boxed—a self-hate thing.

Bobby lived in Jersey City—the armpit of the world. In a national poll, Jersey City was once voted as one of the ten worst places to live in the United States. It's a dung-heap. Bobby was an auto mechanic in Jersey City. And each afternoon after work when he walked into the gym, he had the same black sludge beneath his fingernails—that black sludge *was* Jersey City.

Bobby was old for the Gloves—twenty-six. Twenty-six was the oldest a fighter could be to enter; sixteen was the youngest. Why he waited until his last year, I don't know. Maybe he thought that waiting would give him a psychological edge over the younger kids.

But Bobby's fine muscle tone and stamina were now long gone. After showering, when wet, naked and exposed, he always joked, "Hey! 'Fat' is only a three-letter word invented to confuse people." Fighters laughed at Bobby.

Beneath his gray sweatshirt, Bobby wore the clear plastic bags from the cleaner's that suffocate babies. He wrapped the bags around his body, arms and legs and tied them together with tape. When we sparred, I quickly discovered that because of the plastic, I could hear his punches coming a split-second before he actually threw them. I never told him this. The first time we sparred, I didn't hear soon enough, and he nailed me with his best shot, a lunging right after a body-fake. The punch boomed on my jaw and should have floored me, but I hardly felt it.

I liked Bobby, but he just couldn't punch. As a boxer, Bobby was what Mrs. Simon, my high school English teacher, called *me* as a student—"seriously mediocre."

I always wondered if Bobby felt as inadequate, vulnerable and out of place dancing inside a boxing ring as I felt sitting quietly at a desk in Mrs. Simon's English class. If he did, he didn't show it. He was always cracking jokes. He didn't joke with me, though. I didn't talk much, and I kept to myself. I wasn't in the gym to make friends.

"I think we both got a good chance to reach the finals," said Bobby. Nervousness pinched his voice. "Wouldn't that be something, fighting each other in the Garden?"

I nodded.

Tom and Sal, in the front seat, grunted in effortless sociability. The wind squirmed outside; black raindrops chafed the windows.

"Almost there," said Tom, looking back at me.

I tried not to think. For me, thinking was dangerous. My weakest link was my brain. I had enough problems to prove it. So I shut my brain off.

My brain worries. It fears. It snarls. It forgets. It remembers. It burps.

My brain screams. I can't trust the damn thing. My biceps are much more reliable. Instinct is more effective than thought in a boxing ring, anyway. But as I sat there trying to relax, the bag of my brain was bulging to the brim with hate and fertile excrement. It was my habit to collect all this debris, remember it and store it away for use on my opponent's face.

The wind whirled and squalled outside the car windows as we

approached St. Jude's High School. The urge to nail somebody with a good solid punch didn't really come from my brain or my genes. It sprung from somewhere else. I wasn't a fighter by heredity. My mother was an interior decorator, and my father was a songwriter. I fell somewhere in between. But I found out early that there are not many things in my world other than a candy bar or a good stiff lay that have as much immediate gratification for me as one good solid left hook to a guy's jawbone.

As I sat there staring out at the rain, I didn't think about my mother or my father or my being between them. I thought nothing. Tonight, I simply sat and listened to nervous Bobby Kemmelman. He thrummed his thick fingertips on the front seat. As we drove closer to the high school, I noticed in the bright neon lights that his fingernails were still caked with Jersey City sludge.

I looked out the window. The sky skulked. There were no stars, only the black, negro night. The most terrifying thing about the dark is the monsters we put in it. Squirming gusts of night whistled and squeaked into the car from a small opening in Sal's front window vent. For some reason, that bothered me.

"Shut your window, Sal," I murmured. Sal did, and I listened to Bobby's fingertips.

Tom slowed his Impala and said, "Get ready, you guys, we're here. That's St. Jude's." He pointed to a brick building with steel-meshed windows that resembled cages. My heart jumped into my mouth, but I feigned nonchalance.

Inside my head there was a chained-up pigmy. *He* thought about things but I didn't listen. He must have been screeching like a trapped rat when Tom finally parked the car and opened the trunk, and I reached in for my gear. *"What the hell am I doing here? Why am I doing this? This is ridiculous!"* I'm sure he cried. And he was right.

All the normal kids in my high school were home doing math problems. Or they were practicing their serves on the tennis court or listening to rock 'n' roll in their bedrooms. The little pigmy was right. What was an upper-class kid from New Jersey, who grew up with a Haitian maid, doing in Manhattan wearing a hoody black hat and chewing a toothpick? What was he doing illegally entering a New York City boxing contest?

The Gloves were open only to New Jersey guys living east of the Passaic River—Hoboken, Secaucus, Kearny—scummy places like that. Where I lived—the northern white-collar suburbs—there were no boxers. We watched them on television. If a guy from my area did have a mind to fight, he learned how by sparring in a basement or garage—it was a lot like taking swimming lessons on the kitchen table.

As we walked toward St. Jude's, I made sure I looked tough. I wasn't sneering but I wanted to look as Cro-Magnon as possible. More important, I made sure I held my gym bag in my right hand—I didn't want anyone to know that I was a southpaw. At the entrance, Tom stopped and whispered, "Remember, when you sign in, don't use your own address, use mine. We'll make it look like you live with me."

As I stood in line waiting to register, I didn't waste time looking at the other fighters. I knew that their faces would be twisted into tough-guy sneers—the sneers that they had practiced the previous night. Who needs it? Let them waste precious energy trying to psyche me out. Those types were all scared bunny rabbits inside anyway. The fighters to worry about were the ones with dead-pan expressions. Psychopaths have dead-pan expressions. So did Joe Louis and Sonny Liston. That's the face I put on.

When it was my turn to sign in, I wanted to keep my southpaw status a secret, so I picked up the pencil in my right hand and scrawled my name as best I could. I had practiced writing this way in the back of Mrs. Simon's class when she was reading *Macbeth*. As I wrote down Tom's address, I hesitated a moment, trying to remember the correct street number. When I finished, the official grabbed what I'd written, frowned, looked up and said, "That's some sloppy handwriting you got, boy. Are you illiterate?" I shrugged and walked away. The sneerer behind me, a muscular white dude with a bird tattooed on his chest, looked at me in what appeared to be wide-eyed fear—so did the black sneerer behind him. Somehow, illiteracy in a fighter is very disturbing. Joe Louis and Sonny Liston were illiterate. And now so was I.

The weigh-in was held in the next room—the school lavatory. Again, it was the same scene—more sneering fighters trying to macho it out. When it was my turn to get weighed, I stepped slowly onto the scale. It was damp from everyone's sweaty feet. The needle shot to 163 pounds. Perfect. That's exactly where I wanted to be. At 163, I moved my quickest and punched my hardest. I walked to the dressing room to tell Tom.

A dressing room is a bad place to be. You wait and wait, chasing away negative thoughts. The little seconds seem like little eternities when you're alone in a dressing room. You wind up with a headache in the pit of your stomach. The thought of getting punched in the nose hurts much worse than the actual punch. That's why it's good to deaden your mind into a vegetable. No brain, no pain.

It was about 7:00 P.M. I sat there, stripped to my green nylon boxing trunks and wearing white socks and white wrestling shoes with the rubber soles that provided traction on the canvas when I punched. My fight would be in one or two hours, but I still didn't know who I would face.

"They'll match you up with a chump your own size and weight," said Tom, looking around the room. The dressing room was nothing more than a biology classroom with fighters sitting in it. The other fighters and trainers sat in private clusters.

"You just relax," Tom said loud enough so that the fighters in the closest clusters could hear. "You'll kill any asshole they put in the ring with you. I know you, Pete." He chuckled sadistically. "You'll spit in their faces!" I flinched inside but remained deadpan.

The secret to the Gloves is to maintain your equilibrium. Tom once had told me back in the gym, "If you want to be a fighter,

Pete, the muscles of your soul gotta be strong." And he was right. Since it was an open dressing room, you couldn't help noticing other fighters. Some looked good as they shadowboxed against a wall or snaked swift punches into their trainers' open palms. Some—the ones with cloth gym shorts, tennis sneakers and no gym affiliation—looked bad. And some had such powerful physiques that just looking at them made me nauseous.

I wanted to fight a black guy. I figured that a black would be thinking that just because I was white and he was black, I would be frightened of him. I wanted to spit in his eye and prove him wrong.

Most of the good fighters were black; most fighters anyway were black. However, there was one white guy, a muscular German-looking fighter, who caught my eye. He was shadowboxing on the side. I tried not to stare. He wore baby-blue trunks and high white boxing shoes—the type pros wear. He looked like he'd been around. But this tournament was for the subnovice championship—for inexperienced fighters with no sanctioned A.A.U. fights. With his smashed nose, the U.S.N. tattoo on his biceps and the coolness with which he threw punches, he looked like a Navy champ with a hundred fights.

"He's a ringer," whispered Tom, bandaging my hands with white gauze. "Look at him—he's had a lotta fights. I don't know how that bastard got in this damn tournament." Tom looked worried.

By this time, I didn't care who I fought. I just wanted to get it over with. I looked at the round clock ticking on the wall. Tom left to find out from the posted sheet who I was paired with. I opened and closed my fists, which Tom had finished taping with the maximum amount of adhesive tape allowed by the A.A.U. I concentrated on flexing my right hand for the benefit of anyone watching. It was already 8:40, and I was sick and tired of one certain white fighter, and his Neanderthal trainer, who continually stared and grinned at me.

"Let's go—you're next," said Tom. He sounded out of breath. "You're fighting a white kid named Burns."

* * *

In his corner, twenty-five feet away, stood Joe Burns. I hadn't noticed him in the dressing room. But Tom was right; he looked exactly my size and weight. He glowed with violence as he glared at me from across the ring. It was spooky—with his short brown hair greased with Vaseline and parted in the middle, high cheekbones and stubby nose, he looked enough like me to be myself.

"IN THE RED CORNER," shouted the announcer, "WEIGHING 163½ POUNDS—FROM HASTINGS, NEW YORK—JOE BURNS!" He wore high white boxing shoes, the type pros wear.

"Get loose, move around," Tom instructed as he rubbed my shoulders. I peeked over at Burns as I loosened up. I did what I always did—one at a time, I flailed my arms, clockwise, at my side. Then I punched the air above my head. I'd never seen another fighter do this, but it worked for me. It loosened my back and arm muscles and gave me a longer reach. Plus, it looked apelike.

"IN THE BLUE CORNER," shouted the announcer, "WEIGHING IN AT 163 EVEN, HAILING FROM JERSEY CITY, NEW JERSEY—PLEASE WELCOME 'IRISH' PETE WATT!"

The referee motioned us to center ring. Violence coated Burns' eyeballs. The fight was on as we stared into each other. He didn't flinch. I didn't flinch. Somewhere deep, my pigmy screamed. The packed auditorium began to surge. They sensed blood. Burns deadpanned. I deadpanned.

". . . shake hands and come out fighting." I didn't hear a damn word the referee said.

Back in the corner, Tom spat final instructions. "Move! Jab! See what he's got!"

The bell rang.

Burns ran out fast and attacked. Stunned, I crouched and covered up. His punches were frantic, nervous punches. They hit my gloves and whistled harmlessly overhead. I came up with a left hook. It plopped onto his jaw. Down he went.

I ran to a neutral corner. Everything was happening so fast. "ONE . . . TWO . . . THREE . . . FOUR . . ." Shit, he got up. The ref wiped the resin off Burns' gloves, looked into his eyes and motioned us to fight. Again, Burns rushed. He was trying to prove that his lying on the canvas was a big mistake. It wasn't. He ran into a solid left hook off a jab. He slumped to the canvas. I ran to the same neutral corner.

"ONE . . . TWO . . . THREE." Groggy and red-faced, he looked up at me. I scowled down, hoping to frighten him into quitting. "Stay down, stay down," I silently begged.

"FOUR . . . FIVE . . . SIX . . ." Shit, he got up again. This time, I attacked. He backpedaled, but I was in his chest with lefts and rights. It was all so fast. Suddenly, pinned against the ropes, he ran into a straight right hand. I don't want to brag, but it was a lot like hitting a guy's head with the meat of a baseball bat. Down he went. The referee stopped the fight—the three-knock-down rule—but Burns wasn't getting up anyway. The referee knelt down and removed the mouthpiece from Burns' bleeding mouth so Burns wouldn't swallow it. He laid motionless. Techni-cally, I suppose, he was alive. The crowd screamed. Burns' trainer raced over with smelling salts. Burns slowly began to respond and limply stood up.

Since prehistoric times, man has been enthralled by violence. And every leather-lunged boxing fan in the crowd that night howled his enjoyment. Except for one man. He sat in the last row of the auditorium. Beside him sat the woman who had sewn the green shamrock onto my white robe. As the referee raised my arm and announced me a "TKO winner in 1:02 of the first round," the man sat there quietly with deep, thick worry lines creasing his forehead. I knew this guy, and I loved him. He was a serene man with gray hair and glasses. He was my father. And he was very, very perplexed.

Bobby Kemmelman stood in the bathroom frowning before the mirror.

"Sorry about your fight, Bobby," I said. He shook his head angrily as I patted his red shoulder. It was a horribly acned and lumpy shoulder. He must, I thought, be pretty self-conscious standing inside a ring like that. His skin lost him his fight. The referee had stopped it at the end of the first round due to a cut eye. Ironically, his skin is what had made him fight, and his skin is what had made him lose.

"What pisses me off is that I hurt him early, and he just ran," Bobby said. I looked at the black stitching above his eye. It resembled one thick black pubic hair twisted into his skin.

"How many stitches?"

"Four," he said, shaking his head with disgust. "Jab, jab, jab—that's all this guy did." Bobby raised his hand and voice high into the air, "This guy, Valero, was about six-one—now how am I going to catch a guy six-one if he starts running?"

I shrugged and shook my head.

"He was no fool," Bobby pointed his index finger with all that Jersey City sludge in the tip of it and said, "That son-of-a-bitch Valero ran 'cause I hurt him bad in the belly!" Bobby smiled, content with this spoonful of happiness, and began combing his hair.

I walked to the other side of the lavatory and urinated. Standing there calmly, I realized that this was the first time since I had started training two months ago that I felt relaxed. Watching my warm, yellow stream drain off, I thought how a brain is very much like a penis. In both, elimination brings release.

As I opened the lavatory door, I noticed Bobby inspecting the scalp hairs lying on his hairbrush. He looked at them as if they were little deaths. Walking out, I couldn't help noticing Bobby was picking the hairs from the brush and carefully placing them back on his head.

Heading back to Jersey City, Tom drove down Broadway toward the Holland Tunnel. Unlike before, during the drive to the fight, my senses were now open and free. A fight does that.

On the right, we passed Madison Square Garden.

"You'll be fighting there soon," said Tom, smiling back at me. Since I wasn't too good at mastering the technique of arriving at that tricky spot between self-confidence and cockiness, I simply shrugged.

I had completely annihilated Burns and was a class above a guy like Kemmelman, but I couldn't be too sure about a fighter like Valero or that white Navy guy. It wasn't in the bag yet.

Tom drove me to my house. I hopped out with my duffle bag. "Thanks, Tom," I said tiredly.

"Good fight, Pete. Take tomorrow off. See you in the gym the next day—no roadwork."

"Okay, Tom, thanks—see ya."

As I walked to the front door, my stomach tightened. I opened the front door.

"Hi, everybody. I'm home."

Now was when the real fighting would begin.

TWO

THE FAMILY

Etiquette

The problems all began with Elvis.

I remember one summer evening when I was six years old. I sat with my father in the kitchen listening to music on the radio. Dad couldn't quite enjoy the twanging guitars, the crazy lyrics and the cocky white kid mimicking a black man. It wasn't his thing.

"What is this . . . music?" he asked.

Dad couldn't understand rock 'n' roll. What he could understand was that his own songs weren't selling. Fewer people were buying the slow, melodic ballads. Music was changing.

Home life was changing, too.

Much to my mother's dissatisfaction, Dad was no longer the promising young composer that *Time* Magazine had once exalted.

Each night after crawling home from New York City, he resembled something gooey that had been scraped off the sidewalk.

It had been eleven dry years since his back-to-back smashes had topped the Hit Parade (one performed by the Mills Brothers, the other by Frank Sinatra). Plus his royalty checks were getting smaller and smaller.

And my mom wasn't the young Ford model who was willing to forfeit her dreams and remain a housewife anymore. She wanted a career.

One evening, my mother, growing more and more agitated with my father and the whole damn futility of his efforts snapped, "What have you been doing for eleven years, napping?"

"It'll change," said my father softly. "This rock 'n' roll is too wild. People want *songs*, easy listening. Rock 'n' roll can't last."

But it did last. Two years later, my twelve-year old brother, Dan, raced home clutching a new record album. It was by an English group called The Beatles.

BAAABE! BAAABE! BAAABE!

As the shards of music ripped through my father's eardrums and ricocheted into his brain, his face evolved from perplexity to worry to a wince of pain.

He knew that his own music was a zoot suit, an antiquated piece of yesterday. The roar of his talent had faded. He had been wrong, he had to admit it—rock 'n' roll *was* going to last, and probably a lot longer than his own marriage.

The knockout punch came a year later when I was seven.

Dad had gotten a big break. That evening he received a phone call from his publisher. He was told that his new pop single, "The Little Boy," was scheduled to be sung on "The Tonight Show" by Tony Perolli.

The song's melody was simple, beautiful and enchanting (the tune was my Dad's part).

That evening, Mom, Dad, Dan and I sat up waiting.

"Sshh!" sounded my father as Tony Perolli emerged from behind a curtain. Tony smiled and blew kisses to the audience. His cuff links flashed brightly. Wonderful! Spectacular! My father's song!

But watching closely, one could see that something wasn't quite right. Perolli reached for the microphone and fumbled it.

"Oh, no!" gasped my father.

Perolli began singing:

> I knew a boy, a little boy
> A long, long time ago.
> His eyes were bright,
> His step was . . . uh . . . light,
> His head . . . (?) . . . was all aglow . . .

"I don't even recognize it," said my father.

Perolli tangled himself in the black microphone cord and stumbled.

"I can't believe it," said my father, his voice almost a whisper.

The audience tittered. Perolli giggled. Then, laughing uncontrollably, he dropped the microphone to the floor and shrugged. "Sorry," he slurred, "I forgot the words . . . they were *bleep* anyway!"

The audience screamed.

"*He's* sorry," shouted my mother, "*he's* sorry." She ran out of the room, raced downstairs and drove away in the car.

A half-year later—thanks to Elvis, The Beatles and Tony Perolli—my parents were divorced.

My mom found work in New York City as an interior decorator, and six months after that, she was engaged to a rich New Jersey judge.

I saw my father every other weekend.

This wealthy New Jersey judge had spawned four very screwed-up kids. His youngest son was Lance, ten years old.

The first time I met Lance, I knew I was in big trouble. He was playing alone in a vacant field next to his house.

"Go introduce yourself," said my mother sweetly. "He's a nice boy."

As I walked toward this thing that was to become my stepbrother, I noticed he was bending over, speaking to a rock. I wasn't close enough to hear what he was saying, but it must have been funny because he was chuckling. The rock, however, didn't seem to be laughing that much. Occasionally, Lance would kick it with the side of his Keds high-top sneaker or prod it with a long stick.

Cautiously I approached.

"Do you like food?" Lance asked the rock. Then he poked it with his stick. "Huh? Huh? I asked you a question!" he barked. "Answer me! Do . . . you . . . like . . . food?" He lifted his stick and waited for the rock's reply. Then, with a swing, he jack-nicklaused it past my feet. As it thumped along the dirt, I saw that this rock was covered with fur and red blood. It had eyes and a face. It was the head of a cat.

"A kitten," said Lance. "He scratched me." He leaned on his stick and said, "You must be Peter."

I nodded.

"My name's Lance," he said, swinging his stick. I noticed the tip of it was red and damp.

"Hi," I said.

"Looks like we're gonna be brothers," he said, jabbing at the ground.

"Yeah," I said with fake enthusiasm.

"I'm ten, how old're you?" he asked.

"Eight," I said.

"Well," said Lance, changing the topic, "that cat bit me." He pointed to a small puncture wound on his hand. "We were only playing with it," he said. "I hate cats."

"Me, too," I lied.

He snickered, "But we fixed him. We caught him hiding under a couch. Then we put him under arrest, like a criminal."

I nodded and grinned to make him think I was on his side.

"Then we threw him in jail and set a court date."

"A court date?"

"For his trial," he explained.

I felt scared, but I continued to grin.

"At our trial, we tied him to a chair and held his paw on a Bible. 'Do you swear to tell the truth, the whole truth and

nothing but the truth?' we asked, but the cat kept screeching."
Lance spoke a mile a minute; his thick pink gums glistened with
saliva. He seemed an authority on trials, probably because of his
father, I thought.

". . . after our trial, the judge—that was Rodney—told me—
the jury, to 'Make a decision.' And that's that."

"You killed the cat?"

"The next morning. Hung him."

"*You* killed him?"

"We both did, me and Rodney."

"Then why'd you cut off his head?" I asked.

"Autopsy."

"What's that?"

"That's when you cut someone up to see what made them
die."

"But *you* made him die."

"I know," giggled Lance, "but we cut him up for fun."

"Who cut off his head?" I asked.

"We both did, me and Rodney."

"Who's Rodney?"

"My big brother."

Holy shit, I thought, grinning.

Four hours later, my mother's V.W. Beetle rolled into the
driveway. I ran to the car, hopped in and slammed the door shut.

"How did it go, sweetie?" she asked. She kissed the top of my
forehead gingerly so as not to mess her sticky new hairdo.

"Rotten," I said, rubbing my cheek muscles, which ached
from smiling. Etiquette.

"Rotten? How come?" she asked.

I tried to answer, but couldn't. I was too upset. Jungle-growths
of confusion choked my brain, making it difficult to explain
things like *reasons*. I wanted to tell her about the kitten's head,
the tension radiating from their house, Lance's nose infested with
greasy blackheads, his thick pink gums . . .

Blurting and stuttering, I forgot simple nouns like cat, stick and room. I tried hard to communicate, but only got more frustrated, angry and upset. My mind snagged on simple ideas.

My first grade teacher, Mrs. Long, once had told my mother this was because "Peter has a split-second lag between his mind and his mouth." My mother disagreed. She blamed it all on my dad—he stuttered, too.

"Calm down," she soothed. "Now what was this about a cat?"

Plucking and scrambling for words, I did my best to explain but I finished by blurting, "I hate them all!"

She stared at me with an expression of either concern or disbelief. "Oh, Peter," she said, smiling and gently stroking my hair as if it were fur, "They're pulling your leg. You know, dear, in life you must learn to get along with many types of people. That's why it's good you have your brother Daniel. Sometimes you two fight, but you still love each other . . ."

"Mommy, I don't want Lance to be my brother. I don't want you to marry Mr. Ceffone . . ." Again, jungle-growths choked my thoughts. "They're bad people." I bit my lower lip; there was so much I sensed, knew and understood, but I couldn't find the words.

"Come now," said my mother. "Mr. Ceffone is a very nice man."

"I wish he was never born," I said, grinding my teeth.

"Living with them will be very comfortable. You'll love it, I promise. You'll have a large field to play in—"

"Where would I sleep?" I asked.

"In Lance's room."

"With Lance?"

"Of course."

I winced at the thought. "Where will Daniel sleep?"

"With Rodney."

Grief seemed to rise up my throat. I thought of the kitten's head and Lance's pink gums. I didn't do anything so terrible to deserve this. I was guilty of innocence.

I thought of my father and Mr. Ceffone. They seemed so . . . different. Why couldn't my mother understand that this was all wrong. I disliked them all for no good reason—except the very good one that I felt anger and insincerity oozing from each one of them.

"Don't marry him, Mommy. Please . . . don't marry him."

"Hush now," my mother said. "Everything is set. The wedding is next week."

My heart stopped short. Tears pulsated from my eyes. "Why? Why?" I yelled.

"I'm doing it for you!" she said.

I howled.

"I'm doing it for you *and* Daniel," she added.

"Sure!"

"Please, Peter!" my mother implored. "Calm down."

"You're doing it for yourself!" I turned away and pressed my nose against the window, watching the orange sun slip from the July sky through a prism of tears. "I wish I was dead," I whispered. I felt myself escaping to another place with Sticko, my imaginary Indian friend. Sticko, although Indian, always wore a wide-brimmed cowboy hat, and he was always smiling.

"Come on, you'll love it there," coaxed my mother. "We'll have a maid. And you'll swim in the country club pool."

Sticko and I were playing leap-frog far away.

"It will be a wonderful place to live." said my mother.

Not if you're a kitten, I thought to myself.

I look back at the wedding, and I don't remember a damn thing. I only recall snatches of the reception. It's like I'm watching an old black-and-white movie of myself. The film is grainy, jerky and poorly lit.

I see myself wandering through an enormous country club ballroom. There are tall windows and long velvet drapes. Well-dressed men and women eat chunks of food from toothpicks. They sip drinks. They shake my hand and pat my back. I smile, to be polite. Etiquette. But I'm alone. And for the first time in my life, I'm exquisitely aware of the boundaries of my own skin.

I see starched white tablecloths, silverware and flower bouquets. I stare at the waiters. They appear happy, like me, but their smiles are much too polite and perfumed. I sense that they don't want to be here.

I feel sad. This invisible sadness is like the smell of damp wool within me. It isn't anything special. It is just sadness.

I listen to the band. The music is slow and melodic, like my father's music.

My mother finds me sitting alone at a table. I am looking out the window. Secretly, Sticko, the smiling Indian, and I are crawling into a golf cup on the putting green.

"Having fun?" trills my mother.

I hardly recognize her. She is wearing a white dress studded with sequins, and her hair and face have a waxen appearance. She doesn't look like my mother—she looks more like Ceffone's wife.

I listen to the soft music and wonder what my father is doing at that very minute.

"Come on, grouchy," she says, poking my belly with her long painted fingernail, "Join the fun—Daniel is."

Don't touch me, I think.

"I want everyone to see you dance with Stacie," she says. Stacie is Mr. Ceffone's eight-year-old daughter.

"No!" I say angrily.

"Please?"

"No." I blink off an angry tear and brush it away quickly as it rolls down my cheek.

"Oh please, sweetie—for me?"

"No. This is your wedding, not mine." My eyes bore into her. "And don't call me 'sweetie' anymore."

"It is my wedding, but you're a part of it," she says.

I crawl back into the golf cup with Sticko.

She lowers her head and pouts, "Don't you love me anymore?"

My brain bulges with chaos and confusion.

"Honey," says my mother to someone else, "Peter isn't having a good time."

My body freezes as I notice a man standing behind me—my new stepfather.

"Of course he is!" declares Mr. Ceffone. My stepfather tilts his head forward and says, "You're having a good time, aren't you, son?"

Son!

I shrug.

He frowns. He has an ugly veined forehead. "Of course you are," he says, patting me firmly on the shoulder. "There will be no party-poopers here. At least not at *my* wedding."

I can't look at him; I glare at my mother instead.

"I think it would be nice if Peter and Stacie danced together, don't you?" my mother says sweetly.

My stepfather looks down at me. "You don't have any problems with that, do you?"

I shrug.

His dark eyes glare at me, and I realize that this father, unlike my real father, requires verbal answers. "No," I lie.

"Good. She's waiting for you at that table." He points and his cuff links flash at his wrists. "I told her to wait there for you."

"Pick a nice dance, sweetie," calls my mother.

I turn my head and glare. She is smiling. I want to argue, but snags, jungle-growths and thinktwists entangle me. Plus, I look at my stepfather, and I am chicken.

For the wedding dinner, the four Ceffone kids and Daniel and I sat together. It was Rodney, fifteen; my brother Dan, fourteen; Raquel, thirteen; Lance, ten; and Stacie and I, both eight. Lance, I noticed, had a black eye.

A smiling waiter served shrimp cocktails.

Lance licked a shrimp, then looked at it as if it had licked him back.

"Stop playing and eat," Rodney said.

"All right already," Lance said, his voice whining.

"Little brothers . . . ," said Rodney contemptuously.

Dan laughed knowingly.

Reacting quickly, I popped a shrimp into my mouth and worried about its taste later.

"You're using the wrong fork, stupid," Rodney told Lance.

"Use the smaller fork," instructed Raquel, holding it up.

After finishing his shrimp, Rodney clacked his bowl with a fork for the last traces of sauce, then lapped the sauce off his fork. To show off, he hooked his thumbs together and fluttered his hands like a butterfly around Lance's plate.

"Knock it off!" Lance said.

"Shut up before I give you *another* black eye," Rodney warned.

"You didn't give me a black eye, *Dad* did!"

Rodney continued fluttering his hands. "Yeah, 'cause you lied about finishing your homework."

"So?" Lance tried to think of something more to say, but Rodney made a quick, swooping motion and with one fast dive, whisked away a shrimp.

"Hey, give that back!"

"Make me," Rodney said.

"Leave him alone," Raquel told Rodney. "You wouldn't do that if Father were here."

"Sure I would," Rodney boasted.

"No you wouldn't," chirped Stacie, " 'cause he'd smack you good."

At that point, Lance slowly dropped his chin onto the white tablecloth. He slid his chin forward and kissed his glass of Coke.

Everyone stared.

"Rodney can have my shrimp, but he can't have my Coke," said Lance. He raised his glass and petted it lovingly. He held the glass to his cheek, closed his eyes and kissed it. "I love you," he cooed.

"Are you crazy?" Rodney asked.

Lance shrugged.

"No," said Rodney, "you're not crazy—you're mentally re-tarded!"

"Stop that!" ordered Raquel.

"He is!" insisted Rodney. "Lance's mentally retarded, just like Uncle Henry."

I glanced at Uncle Henry sitting in the corner. He was a two-hundred-and-sixty-pound man who wore a bib.

"Retard!" Rodney sung out.

"What?" Lance said.

"Why're you always saying 'what'?" Rodney asked.

Lance pulled a face.

"I know why," said Rodney, "because you're retarded."

"Am not," Lance countered.

"You're mental!" Rodney said.

"What?"

"See! There you go again!"

"Naw, it's just that . . . I hear you, but . . ."

"You need time to think. You think slow. That's retarded." Rodney looked at Daniel proudly as if he'd proven an important psychological fact.

"It's a habit," explained Lance. "My friends do it, too."

"I know, because they're retards, too."

"I can break it," sniffed Lance.

"No, you can't."

"Sure I can—just like I did when I sucked my finger."

"Do you know *why* you sucked your finger?"

"Why?"

"Because you're retarded!" Rodney said triumphantly.

Raquel leaned forward. "You'd better stop it right now."

Rodney waved her off like a gnat. "I spoke with Uncle Henry today. Know what the first thing he said to me was?"

"What?" asked Lance.

"That's right!" Rodney said, beaming at his own cleverness.

"What?" repeated Lance.

"He said 'what'!"

"So?" said Lance, glancing at Daniel and me with embarrassment.

"So you're *both* retards!"

"Am not! And if I was, why didn't Dad tell me, huh?" shot Lance.

"Because he's embarrassed by you."

Flustered, Lance knocked over his glass. Coke splashed out, and ice cubes rumbled across the table.

"See, I told you," Rodney said.

Raquel banged her fist on the table. "You two had better stop it right now before Father finds out!"

Stacie giggled nervously.

I glanced nervously at Daniel, who was glancing nervously at Rodney. I could tell that living with these people was going to be as exciting as a broken arm.

"You're a sickie," Rodney said, once again addressing Lance.

"Yes, I'm a sickie," croaked Lance. Then he slumped into his chair as if dead.

Raquel appeared ready to cry. "If you don't stop it, I'm telling Father and I don't mean maybe."

Lance suddenly jumped back to life.

"That's better!" Raquel said.

Glaring, Rodney turned to Raquel, "Hey! Who are you, our mother?"

Everyone froze. Their mother was lying in a cemetery vault, dead of cancer.

Suddenly, Lance reached into a snack food bowl, picked out a plump raisin and wedged it into his nostril. "Look! I'm a sickie!" He blew out the raisin into the palm of his hand, picked it up, examined it and popped it into his mouth.

Everyone gagged.

"A boogie!" he said, chewing triumphantly.

Beneath the table, I anxiously twisted my napkin into a tight knot, trying desperately to conjure up my friend, Sticko, the Indian.

So, I said to myself, as I walked into the house after my first Golden Gloves fight with Burns, you assholes will pretend to be interested in how I did. You'll smile phony smiles and shake my hand, but I know that you bastards secretly wanted me licked. I know it. Who's kidding whom? Your faces are masks. I know what you think about me. After all these years of phoniness, tiptoeing around with etiquette and deception, after all those polite, perfumed pretenses, you will expect me to chitchat with you in your family room. I don't, I didn't, and I never will want anything to do with you. What I feel for you goes deeper and beyond hate!

Yeah. I have an attitude. You were inflicted on me like a disease. My mother wanted you. The bitter taste of ten perverted years lingers in my mouth. But I'm fighting you. You will never stain me. You'll never taint my soul! Never! Because I'm a fighter!

"Hi, everyone," I said with fake politeness, stepping into the family room. "I won!"

THREE

THE SECOND FIGHT

The Muse of Violence

5:00 P.M.

Tom's Impala, with its rusted-out muffler, growled through the Lincoln Tunnel. The car, like him, was dented, scarred and battered like an old punch-drunk fighter.

We were on our way to my second Golden Gloves fight at Holy Cross High School in Queens.

"Your parents coming tonight?" asked Tom.

"Father is," I said softly, cutting out the unnecessary words to conserve energy. I looked out at the squalid tiles of the polluted tunnel and added, "Stepfather might come, too."

Tom snickered. "You got a lot of fathers." He peeked over at me with his crazy, cockeyed face and his eye that always stared upward and said, "You like him, your stepfather, you like him?"

Why was he asking me this? What was I supposed to say— "Well, Tom, I didn't like my stepfather when he got drunk last month and tried to stab my mother in the head." So I ignored him. But still, the evidence throbbed in my mind. I saw it—a big fucking scissor hole in their mattress. My second Golden Gloves fight was a few hours away, and we, my brain and I, were having a bitch getting ready. I didn't want to talk, or think, about a scissor hole or my family. Some family. Thinking about that stuff only messed me up more. A boxer's mind, like his eyes, has to be focused on one thing or else he starts thinking double.

But Tom wanted to know.

"Huh? You like him, you hate him, or what?" He peeked over again, "Stepfathers, I know, can suck."

"He's okay," I said, shrugging. I was concentrating on other things, like not breathing the exhaust fumes that were leaking into the car—they aren't so good for your brain. Plus, I was trying to remember my double jab tonight. The jab flitted in and out of my thoughts, and then suddenly I was back there sneaking into my parents' bedroom. I opened the door, which was always closed, and tiptoed to their bed. I saw a jagged tear in the bedcover. The satin bed sheets were ripped. I snuck closer and inspected the mattress. I stared at the scissor hole. It was clean and deep. I stuck my finger into it. It went in all the way. "Why?" I asked myself.

"I hated my stepfather, too," Tom crowed.

"Didn't say I hated him," I said.

"You said it, all right," Tom said. He steered his piece of shrapnel out of the tunnel.

I guess the truth was in my voice. I *did* hate him. I had now lived with my stepfather and his low-quality family for ten low-quality years. Technically, I suppose they were human beings, but I always thought of them as dirtbags. There was more violence—emotional and physical—in one room of my stepfather's two-hundred-thousand-dollar home than in one dirty city block in Harlem. It had a way of affecting you if you lived there.

There was silence for a while, then Tom said, for no apparent reason, "Pete, did I ever tell you that you remind me of an animal?"

5:30 P.M.

An animal?

As we hit Manhattan, I was trying to escape into sleep. I hated myself for closing my eyes; it was too much like running away, but Floyd Patterson and Joe Louis had done it, too, so I told myself it was okay.

I caught myself thinking about animals. I always thought New York kids were animals—probably the toughest beasts in the world. Look where a lot of them came from: ghettos, slums, barrios. They stole, joined gangs and did drugs. Fighting to them meant chains, knives and zipguns. To New Jersey suburban kids, fighting meant wrestling.

I tried, like Floyd Patterson and Joe Louis, to sleep. But it was thin sleep. Quietly, I concentrated on moves. (Right to the body, left to the head; left to the head, right to the body; whatever I do, do it fast; stay loose; pick my spots; double jab . . .)

"Hey, I got something for you," Tom said. I blinked my eyes open and saw the signs—Thirty-second Street and Ninth Avenue. At the red light, Tom grabbed something from his shirt pocket and handed it to me. I saw that it was a clipping from the sports page of the New York *Daily News.*

"Read it," he said, "the last paragraph."

It was a clipping about my first fight. I read:

> Peter Watt, a Jersey City school boy, representing Brandy's Gym, was impressive in his first bout. Watt packs a potent left hook. With the savagery of an animal he flashed it three times in the opening round to topple another tough hombre, Joe Burns, from Hastings, N.Y. The time was 1:35.

"I knocked him down with the right hand," I said. It peeved me to realize that now all the fighters would figure out that I was a converted southpaw.

"Don't worry—you won. You got ink. What did I tell ya? Kid, you're an animal—they even said it!" He punched my arm playfully. "Hey! And that ain't all. You even got your picture on the back page."

I looked at him.

"In the glove compartment," Tom said. "I didn't wanna wrinkle it."

I flipped open the glove compartment, took out a folded *Daily News* and turned to the back page. There I was. *Me*. Me, in black and white, nailing Burns with a sweeping left hook. I looked awkward, but hell, I looked powerful. Burns's white mouthpiece was knocked into the air, his eyes were rolled up into his head and he was out cold as the camera caught him slumping to the canvas.

Tom was hopping up and down in his seat. "Kid, you're a **killer**. That left hook'll make us famous. I ain't never seen an amateur with a hook like that."

I could tell we were getting closer to Holy Cross High School; everything Tom was saying now was carefully designed to pump me up; I could tell. But I listened.

"You're going to win tonight, I know it," he said, "cause you're an animal." He gritted his teeth and punched at the air as if he were the one fighting. "They'd better dread you. They all read that article and saw your picture and they're pissin' in their pants. You're the one to beat, and they know it!"

I wondered. Something was missing, deep inside me. In the gym, I had trained like a dog. I had even sparred with Mudbone Hopkins, last year's amateur champ. I trained hard, sparred hard and ran hard, but for some reason, I couldn't feel it. Deep inside, something was trembling, rattling. It's hard to think you can win if you know that you can't.

As usual, I was working my brain to the bone with anxiety.

"Mind if I turn on the radio?" I asked. Joe Frazier and Muhammed Ali probably listened to the radio, too, I told myself.

"Sure, go ahead, Champ," said Tom.

I gritted my teeth tightly and forced myself to be calm.

Be calm. Try to relax.

But I knew that out there, somewhere, some ghetto-punk-dirtbag wanted to beat my face into Jell-O. I felt the back of my testicles shrivel up. Shit! I hated myself even more when that happened. You can't fight with your balls cringing and twinging. Any fighter not arriving at a fight knowing he's going all the way isn't worth his weight in feathers. A fighter who is just interested in surviving is going to get hurt, and deserves it.

6:00 P.M.

Tom turned off the music—*Santana.*

I yawned. It was six o'clock and already it was dark. I looked around. The cages on the high school windows glistened in the moonlight. With my duffle bag strategically clutched in my right hand, I walked with Tom up the white stone steps into Holy Cross High School. Actually, I was relieved that we were finally there because inside, on the left, was a bathroom. Calmly, I walked in and took one hell of an uncalm piss. And I pissed all over my hand doing it.

6:30 P.M.

"My name is Robinson!" shouted a thick, muscular black guy, "and I'm gonna kick some asshole's ass tonight—that's for shit-sure!"

This Robinson guy looked like he could do it. He resembled an African beast. As he strutted himself, and his muscles, into the bathroom, I secretly thought that if he hit me, I would definitely start bleeding. I looked at Tom, who was smiling.

"Guy's crazy," he said as he swiveled his finger around his thick cauliflowered ear. Then he resumed wrapping my sweating hands with the white adhesive. The back of my testicles crawled like before.

"Nervous?" asked Tom. "Nervous" was the same as "scared." Fighters and trainers prefer the word "nervous."

I swept the worry under my face like dirt under a rug and shook my head. Fear is a complicated thing to describe. You can't say that it's three feet long and two feet wide or that it weighs twenty pounds or that it's colored bright red or it sounds like a saxophone or it smells like cheese. Fear is a shriveled-up testicle.

I had wanted to be a fighter ever since I was twelve years old when my dad told me stories about fighters like big Jack Johnson with his large, bald head and vicious Mickey Walker, the Toy Bulldog. Now, here I was—I was the fighter, and deep inside, someone was crying, "Get me out of here!"

6:40 P.M.

I always wanted to be alone before a fight. I didn't want to talk to Tom, or friends, or be comforted by them. I just wanted to be alone. I used that time to get psyched. There's a lot of pressure. I had trained two weeks (and nine years before that) just to spend six minutes—or less—tonight with one of the toughest street punks in the city. Some guy like Robinson, maybe.

One of the Gloves officials, a bald guy, walked over to me and inspected my taped hands. After he felt them and was satisfied, he took out his red felt-tipped pen and scribbled "X"'s on each hand.

Just then, Robinson barged out of the bathroom and stalked into the dressing room. Everyone stared at his rear end. Streaming from beneath his gold satin trunks, dangling down the back of his leg, was a long piece of toilet paper. Suddenly, some guy shouted out, "I ain't never seen a black monkey with no white tail before!" I looked over and saw that the voice ricocheted from the mouth of that white Navy dude with the tattoo and the baby-blue trunks.

"What you say, white boy?" growled Robinson as he slowly walked over. The Navy guy angrily bounced up. His fists were balled, and his blue eyes were snapping like firecrackers.

"I said, black boy, that my name is Gillio, and I think you suck dogs!" Any second, fists would fly. Everyone was quiet. But Robinson, scared, backed down. Instead of doing anything real, Robinson snickered and shot off five or six silly muscle-bounded punches into the air. Then he walked away quickly. The white toilet paper fluttered in the air behind him.

6:50 P.M.

The dressing room air was damp, heavy and tense, and it was difficult to breathe. Damn asthma. The thought that I didn't want to be there crawled dangerously close to the surface. The balls of my feet and hands were sweating, and it vaguely occurred to me that if I won my fight tonight, I'd have to go through this whole damn dressing room thing again.

Absolutely the first essential step toward becoming a champion fighter is to decide that you really want to do it. Beware of what you want, because you might get it.

I was a hair in my own eye. I sat there stewing in anxiety. To be a good boxer you must step fully into the role of a carnivorous monster, but tonight I was having a hard time. Plus, I had developed a habit of burping. Nerves.

Tom looked up, grinned and said, "Miguel, he burped before his fights, too."

"Huh," I said, nodding my head. Miguel Barahona, "The Jersey City Jolter," was Tom's pet pug. Miguel, a Cuban club fighter in the late fifties, fought a few middle-weight contenders, but always lost the big ones. Miguel was a slugger, and he wasn't all that good, but Tom thought he was. And to Tom, I was his new Miguel; his new "Jersey City Jolter."

"Tonight, you just keep punchin'—like Miguel. In these three-round fights, there ain't much room for prettiness—just plug. The judges like the guys who go ape-shit."

I listened to Tom speak. I listened and nodded and belched.

I didn't want to end up looking like Miguel; fat flabby nose and all. No thank you. Besides, the mark of a good fighter is not having marks. I knew Miguel. Sometimes he hung around the gym, and you could see he was punch-drunk. He lost his balance walking, and he slurred words. I wasn't Miguel; I was me, whoever that was. Miguel was brain-damaged. I suppose, I, too, was brain-damaged, but not like punch-drunk. My brain damage was emotional damage from other things.

But I listened to Tom as he spoke. I listened and nodded and belched.

7:30 P.M.

"I'm checkin' to see if you're posted yet," said Tom, anxiously. As he stood up, he added, "Yeah, Champ, I'm gonna go see who you're gonna knock out tonight." He said it loud enough so other fighters and trainers could hear. My head was down, and I felt my heart and every hair on my head lurch up. I fought the urge to look at the Navy guy, Gillio. I knew exactly where he was sitting. I promised myself not to look . . . but I looked anyway. He was staring dead at me and smiling. I coughed and spit on the concrete floor. Burping, I felt more like a raw ganglion than a fighter. Pops of sweat grew on my forehead, and the back of my testicle shriveled even tighter. To break the tension, I stood up, swiveled my neck and calmly walked to the bathroom to piss. I told myself that I had to go anyway.

In the bathroom, a flabby brown smell slapped my nose. A memory flashed back; when I was three. I remembered tottering into our bathroom after my mother had used it. The same ugly brown stink had slapped my nose then, too—plus there was an awful, meatlike vaginal stench. That was my mother! I was surprised that she was capable of such a thing. My own mother! But I still loved her. Today, though, you couldn't smell her if you tried. You smell a perfume bottle—that expensive French shit my stepfather buys her. They're both dirtbags.

For a moment I wished that I could rub my mother's nose in what I was looking at—a puddle of puke. Someone's lunch from someone's stomach. It would have smacked her back into reality. It lay thickly on the floor next to a toilet. I grinned, knowing that one of these tough guys upchucked. The puke consisted of hot dog chunks, beans and milk; a ghetto boy's meal. I was relieved to see one solid sign that I wasn't the only nervous asshole around here.

As I walked out the bathroom door, I hated myself. I angrily thought how pathetic I was for needing a puddle of puke to help build confidence.

7:45 P.M.

"We drew a longhair," Tom said.
"What?"
"Get ready, we're fightin' a hippie named Compo."
Tom smiled confidently and pointed at a long-haired white kid bouncing up and down in the dressing room. Tom considered all longhairs sissies; but I wasn't so sure. Some guys with ponytails in our high school were pretty tough—and this Compo had a damn good build. I remembered seeing Compo earlier at the weigh-in. With his broken nose, I thought that he looked like Jack Palance, the actor. I also noticed that Compo didn't smile much.

Suddenly, Tom gasped. "Oh, shit!" His eyes bulged. "Look, he's a lefty." I watched Compo shadowbox. He *was* a lefty. I never had fought a southpaw before. Well, I would now.

"Let's go," I mumbled, "I don't give a shit."

8:00 P.M.

There were two metal chairs inches apart. Raphael Compo sat on one, me in the other. We fought next. Tom whispered advice into my ear, but the truth about boxing is that it's like dying, you have to do it alone. I sat there chewing the inside of my cheek. I thought about the correct strategy for fighting a southpaw. I knew the way to beat a lefty was with your right hand—but my right hand was my weakness. This fight was up for grabs.

Except for the distant screams of the crowd, there was a

pungent quietness. I concentrated on what Tom had said earlier, "You're the one to beat—they'd better dread you—they're pissing in their pants." I repeated it over and over again, but I wasn't convinced. The Muse of Violence just wasn't there.

Sitting inches from Compo, I suppressed all burps and yawns. Except one. I burped one Primo Carnera burp. I hoped that his mind would interpret it as nonverbal disdain. Hitting a fighter in the brain is sometimes more effective than hitting him on the head. You can do this safely because you don't even have to be in the ring to do it. But Compo's legs only swayed slowly back and forth. I remember thinking confidence is a good sedative.

A lecture that my English teacher, Mrs. Simon, had given, popped into my head. It was about suffering. She said "Suffering is a noble and wonderful thing. It teaches a person about life." Well, I was sitting there suffering my ass off, and as far as I was concerned, suffering is overrated—it doesn't teach a damn thing. She could shove it.

A Gloves official trotted into the room. He looked at his clipboard and shouted, "Watt and Compo—you're on!"

We both stood and loosened up. A thin smile broke at the corners of my lips; I wondered what Compo would have done if he had known that he was going to fight a guy who was a former bed-wetter.

8:10 P.M.

I bobbed and pranced down the aisle—the way I saw pros like Joe Frazier do it on television. Tom followed with towels and water bucket. The crowd, seeing Compo and me, began to applaud; it wasn't the well-bred applause of a tennis match. Their yells ripped the smoky air—already they were drooling with excitement.

As I jogged up the ring steps and dipped through the red felt ropes into the ring, I felt tired and weak. I sensed my spirit sag and the sinews of my soul twitch. To make matters worse, the canvas was thick and soft, and as my wrestling shoe sank into it I felt like I was stepping into a sandbox.

8:25 P.M.

"IN THE BLUE CORNER—AT 163 POUNDS—HAILING FROM JERSEY CITY, NEW JERSEY—WITH A RECORD OF ONE KNOCKOUT—IRISH PETE WATT!"

I ignored the cheering crowd. They were nice, but it meant nothing. James J. Corbett, the heavyweight champion in 1897, ignored the crowd, too. It disgusted him to find out, when he won the crown, that the people who congratulated him the most were the same ones who earlier had screamed for his blood.

I tried to escape into the center of my thoughts. I flailed my arms with my ape-man routine, but I felt like a fake. There I was, inside a boxing ring, a person disguised as a fighter. I felt like the white guy in *Black Like Me* who darkened his skin and traveled in the South so he could experience firsthand what it was to be black.

"Come here, kid," yelled Tom, "Grease you up." On his fingertips was a glob of Vaseline.

"IN THE RED CORNER," bellowed the announcer, "AT 164½—FROM QUEENS, NEW YORK—WITH A RECORD OF ONE KNOCKOUT—RAPHAEL COMPO!" Compo, unlike me and James J. Corbett, acknowledged the crowd by raising his hands and smiling.

Tom wiped the Vaseline on my eyebrows and high cheekbones. The rest he wiped on my arms.

"Relax! Relax!" he said, rapidly puffing his old-man breath into my Vaselined cheeks. "You're gonna knock this hippie out. Bell rings, you can run across the ring and you **nail** him."

The bell clanged, and the referee motioned to Compo and me. As I walked to ring center, I watched my shoes sink into the soft canvas. I thought that if my head hit this, it wouldn't be too bad. I wasn't afraid of getting knocked out, it's just that I didn't want to be there when it happened.

I promised myself to stare into Compo's eyes during the ref's instructions. That's tougher than it sounds. If a fighter looks close enough, he can see emotion on an eyeball. I wanted to see what was lurking inside Compo. I was hoping to see in him the nervousness that I felt in myself.

The referee started his introduction—no one ever listens to that crap. But Compo was. He kept nodding his head as if he were actually listening. He still hadn't looked at me. Finally, the ref finished his chitchat with Compo.

"Shake hands and come out fighting."

Compo raised both gloves to shake. I wouldn't have it. I stepped back. He stepped toward me. Again, he tried to shake hands. This time he looked at me with his broken-nosed face. It was, I saw, a scared face, and his wide brown eyes were coated with fear. I turned and walked to my corner.

The crowd was yelling, Tom was yelling and my mind was yelling, and the strangest thing was, I didn't hear a damn thing. I was still seeing Compo's eyes.

At the bell, the icy snowball in the pit of my stomach burst, and my mind floated away serenely, like a butterfly.

8:40 P.M.

Compo, his broken nose, his shoulder-length hair and his scared eyes met me halfway at middle ring. Chin tucked in safely behind my shoulder, I advanced. I was thinking nothing. And if anybody tells you that he's thinking this or that at a time like this, he is a damn liar.

I feinted with my knees, I feinted a right and waited. I had this mental thing—I always waited till my opponent threw the first punch, even if it was only a jab. I wanted him to start the shit off. I had promised God that I'd never start a fight, and if I did, somehow, I knew that he would get me beat up. Throwing the first punch was too much like being the instigator. I've had over two hundred street fights (I counted them one night lying in bed), and not once had I started a fight, and not once had I lost a fight (except, maybe, against some of the older guys).

I moved to the left, away from Compo's power hand, and waited. Compo, gloves up, moved closer and threw some shots, jabs—right-handed jabs. He missed. The fight was on.

I joe-fraziered toward Compo. I didn't know what, but I felt something, I sensed something. Boxing, like higher math, transcends language. As I weaved closer, he hit me on the forehead with three quick jabs, but I gave him that. I wanted to move closer. Like Max Schmeling studying the films of a young Joe Louis, "I saw somezing."

I saw an opening. Compo's weakness was whispering to me. I don't know how, but because of his lefty stance, there was an angle—an angle in which I could land not the right hand, but the left hook! But Compo must have sensed it, too, because he stepped back. A little at a time, I moved in again behind my jab, not trying to land, just jabbing. But, again, Compo escaped. The crowd was yelling. He jabbed and let go a left. Nothing. It sailed over my shoulder. Now he was close. I shot out two little nimble jabs to set him up. Then I stepped in low and threw it—the left hook. I felt my power lunge from the ball of my foot to my shoulder to my fist to the flesh on his face. The hook blurred through the air and whacked onto the right cheek. Down he went.

"ONE . . . TWO . . . THREE . . ."

He fumbled on the canvas. Saliva dripped from his mouth. My heart, brain and arteries were pounding. The crowd's screams pounded into my eardrums.

"SEVEN . . . EIGHT . . ."

Compo stood up—but not wisely. The ref wiped his gloves and peered into Compo's eyes. Compo nodded. The referee waved us to continue. Compo was hurt. His eyes were popping out, wild and dazed. Frantically, he danced away. Frantically, I chased. He tried to keep me off, but his punches were limp.

And the angle was still there. I crouched low, faked to the body and came up with another hook. The punch sunk into his jawbone as if his bone were butter.

He crashed to the canvas.

"ONE . . . TWO . . . THREE"

Compo's body sprawled out on the canvas and oozed slowly, like a cracked egg.

"FOUR . . . FIVE . . . SIX . . ."

Slowly, he crawled to his knees. His long hair dangled into his eyes.

"SEVEN . . . EIGHT . . . NINE" He blinked at the referee, stood up and nodded his head.

The crowd, shrieking, wanted their kill. I wanted my kill, and Compo wanted to be killed. The ref again motioned us to fight.

I raced out of the neutral corner. I realized that I needed one more knockdown to end the fight. One more punch, just one more, and this shit would be over. I lunged with a left, it missed Compo's nose by inches. He wobbled back. Just one more, just one. I shot off a straight right, it missed his ear by inches. Just one. Desperately, he backpedaled. Mouth open, he rasped for air. Again, I lunged. He arched back, but this time, his tired, scrambling feet stumbled on the soft canvas. He tumbled through the ropes, onto the floor, and landed halfway out of the ring. Chasing, I tripped over his white Everlast shoes and pounced directly on top of him.

Intimidation is a big thing in boxing, so I opened my mouth, bared my mouthguard (that I originally used for football) and growled. Inches away was his face staring back at me, red and sweaty. I'm pretty nonverbal, so I didn't say, "Fuck you!" or "I'll kill you, you pussy!" I just twisted my face and growled. I could have nailed him, too, but I didn't Everyone was yelling, the referee struggled to pry me off Compo and flashcubes exploded with light—it was a circus. Ringsiders shoved Compo back into the ring—they wanted their kill—but the bell rang. The round was over, and Compo was saved.

"What the hell you tryin' to do, get disqualified?" yelled Tom as he scrambled into the ring.

"I tripped," I gasped as I sat down on my stool.

"Don't trip!" he yelled as he grabbed my mouthpiece from my mouth. "Finish him off," he ordered. Then he jammed my mouthpiece back in.

I breathed deeply. Asthma. The ten-second buzzer sounded.
"SOUNDS OUT!"
The bell clanged.
The referee should never have let the fight continue. But he
did. Like the white on rice, I was on Compo, hammering his face
with lefts and rights. It felt nice, like I was smashing windows
or something. Down Compo went. As he lay on the canvas, he
seemed to dissolve and disintegrate. The crowd was screaming.
Compo curled into a fetal position, and the blood and saliva from
his mouth dripped onto the canvas like human syrup. Lying
there, Compo resembled pounded meat with long hair and a
broken nose. I wonder what he would have said had he known
that his ass had just been kicked by a former bedwetter—a
bedwetter who also had sucked his thumb.

9:10 P.M.

"THE WINNER—BY A KNOCKOUT IN TWENTY SEC-
ONDS OF THE SECOND ROUND—PETE WATT!"
That's when the shit started. The lousy crowd began booing.
Booing *me!* They thought I was a dirty fighter or something. I
looked out at them; their screams squirted into the smoky air.
I couldn't believe it. I had just given these morons what they all
wanted—their lousy kill—and now they were bellowing at me
because I had given it to them. My mind began to jump and
thrash wildly as I stood half-naked in the middle of the ring. I
stood there helpless, and I hated these hard-core entertainment
fans for making me helpless. Two seconds ago, I was invincible.
James J. Corbett was right about crowds.
The anger and hate in my head began to spasm with the relief
that I felt after the fight. I felt like I was going mental. The bald
truth is that I was going crazy.
Smiling, I bounded over to Tom and planted a big fat kiss on
his sweaty forehead.
"What the fuck you doin'?" he shouted.
"Fanning the fucking flame!" I hollered back.

The crowd, seeing the smile on my face, got madder and booed even louder. That's exactly what I wanted.

Eyes popped out and grinning, I ran to the middle of the ring and began slipping every single asshole in the crowd the finger. It didn't make much sense because my gloves were still on, but I think they got my message. They booed frantically. I loved it.

I hated them, and I loved hating them. At the top of my lungs I started screaming, "Fuck you! Fuck you!" I hoped that the other fighters were watching. I was getting more and more rapid, sicker and sicker, and I wanted them to see what they were dealing with if they were going to fight me. The message was: I'm crazy.

The crowd was shrieking, and by now the very protons of my brain were hot and canine. Fried brain. I should have been put on a leash, but the referee jumped out of the ring.

"Pete! Pete!" screamed Tom. He tried to grab me but I threw him aside. The ring bell clanged wildly; I ignored that, too. Like a demented baboon, I paced around the ring. Looking at me, it would have been easy to presume that I wasn't a human being. I didn't feel like one, I felt like an animal—the animal that Tom said I was. My eyes, bulging, had the intensity of two black holes in space. There I was, staring out of myself. There was more where this came from—there was a whole lot more. There was ten years of unfinished chaos in my head, just waiting and squirming.

The other fighters . . . I hoped that they were watching. I'm sure they were. They might come from the ghetto, but I *was* a ghetto. I am a ghetto, I told myself. A walking, breathing, screaming ghetto!

9:55 P.M.

In the hallway after the fight, my father stared at me worriedly as if I were something zoological.

"When I saw you fighting tonight," he said, "I saw a stranger. I didn't see my son, I saw someone else."

My father was always worrying. Worry was his best emotion. "Are you okay?" he asked, peering at me with that damn frightened expression of his.

"Of course I am," I said, combing my wet hair with my fingers. "It was all an act, Dad, don't worry. I'm okay."

But I wasn't okay. Some people walk around with pneumonia, walking pneumonia, and don't know it. I was in the middle of a good nervous breakdown, and I didn't know it.

I looked at my father's frightened face; sometimes it seemed as if I fought because I didn't want to grow up to become like that frightened face. Still, no one saw inside my father's face like me. Everyone else just saw a worried man with white-gray hair; they saw a man staring out of large black-framed glasses and breathing through a large Jimmy Durante nose. Me, I saw more.

I saw a man who, as a little boy growing up in England, was thrilled to meet his own father. But they only met once; the second time, his father never showed up at the park bench. I saw a man who smiled happily when he picked up his own son every other weekend in his white Dodge. I saw a man who could have been his father's echo and deserted his son and been nothing more to him than a memory of a thin, flat Kodachrome.

I lived for those weekends with my father.

Just being with my own father was a luxury because the rest of the time I lived with my mother and a phony father and his screwy family. Living with these people was in truth not living; it was scarcely even existing. For ten years, I felt different, like a black dog being raised by a white hog. That's abnormal.

Fighting—the way I fought—might be abnormal, too, but an abnormal reaction to an abnormal situation is not abnormal behavior.

Suddenly, a black guy wearing a green army jacket and a pair of black leather pants ran up to us. My father, frightened, shied away. The guy grabbed my hand and shook it.

"Man, you're some fighter!" he said pumping my hand. "You jus' like ma idol, Muhammed Ali! Shit! You're ma man! I's followin' you into the finals!" Then he raced down the corridor and out the door. My father and I looked at each other and smiled. His smile, I noticed, was a real smile, strained, but real. And there was, I also noticed, a piece of pride in that smile, too.

10:05 P.M.

My duffle bag was clutched as a righty would clutch it—in my right hand. I looked up at the negro color of night and turned up my collar. A lone star twinkled in the distance like a beauty mark in the sky. As we walked to my father's car, my father pointed and whispered, "See that guy over there?" I looked across the street and recognized him immediately. It was Robinson, the muscular fighter with the toilet-paper tail. He and a girlfriend hopped across the street towards us. I could see that he was wearing one of those Muslim skullcaps.

"Wow! Did he get clobbered!" whispered my father. As Robinson and his lady friend walked by us, I faintly overheard him grumble something about "not feeling good" and "a shit-ass hot dog." I smiled to myself, remembering the puke on the floor. As they walked far enough away, my father whispered, "Pete, I have never in my life seen anything like it. I'm surprised he's walking. He got hit so hard, both his feet left the floor." Again, he looked at me with his damned worried expression and added, "He fought a fellow named Abe Griffith—I hope to God you don't have to fight him. He's not human."

I looked at those damn worry lines creasing Dad's forehead. Don't tell me that, Pop, I don't want to hear it! I had to avoid my father's fear and lack of confidence. Something in my mind had begun to gel—something I'd been waiting for . . .

I'm going to win this Golden Glove Championship, I told myself. They'd better dread me because . . . I'M THE ONE TO BEAT.

And this time, when I said it, I felt it.

The only one who can beat me, I told myself, is *me*.

That's the Muse of Violence.

FOUR

THE SCHOOL

The Bowery Bum

It was last-period English and I was gazing out of the frosted window of the trailer that our school used as a temporary classroom. Quietly, I watched the falling snow scatter and scramble in the sky. Outside, it was a freezing February day buried in lumps of winter snow, but inside Mrs. Simon's classroom, it was hot, stuffy and stinky. I glanced down at my sneakers and realized that the thick, fetid smell was me. Cheesy fumes wafted from my feet, through my socks and out of the rips of my cloth high-top Cons. Since entering the Golden Gloves three weeks ago, my feet were continually damp with sweat. Even in bed when I woke up, the sheets were warm and moist with perspiration. I hoped no one else could pinpoint the source of the smell.

As Mrs. Simon paced up and down the front of her classroom lecturing about the assignment we were to have read that day, *Macbeth,* I gazed at the tight bun twisted severely onto the back of her head. Mrs. Simon was tough. I always got the impression that she wanted to be tough like Betty Friedan, whom I always felt tried to be tough like the former heavyweight champion John

L. Sullivan, who once had said, "I can whip any man in the house!"

I had enough toughness already from Mr. Sgro, my football coach, and Tom, my boxing trainer, and my stupid stepfather. I didn't want any more in Mrs. Simon.

"In *Macbeth,*" she said, peering out at her class, "Shakespeare reveals the tragedy that befalls a person who elects to follow a course . . ." I glanced at the round black-numeraled clock ticking slow seconds. It read 2:10. Miles away, my thoughts twirled and swirled inside my head, and they had nothing to do with *Macbeth* or Shakespeare. In one and one-half hours, I'd be in Brandy's Gym, fighting. I gulped back the thought of Mudbone Hopkins, my sparring partner. We were going six rounds. Big shit, I said, trying to convince myself. That's how you get good. My girlfriend, Valerie, floated into my mind. I pushed her back, too—she was much too tender and beautiful to deal with now. I couldn't let myself get soft about anything, because, well, I just wasn't that type of dude—I was a fighter.

From the back row, where I was slouching, I looked at the other kids and wondered if they were listening or wandering inside private dreams, like me. What did they think about? What did they want to be? Secretly, I wondered what they thought of me. Who did they see when they looked at me? Did they see me as the same kid who, many years before, had been elected "Most Popular"? Or did they now see a different person—a person who hid in the back row?

I looked at the backs of their heads and wished I were one of them. Someone like . . . Edward Duffield, a violin player—an anonymous short-haired square with glasses and no reputation. He didn't have anything to prove, and he didn't know the beast named Mudbone Hopkins, and he didn't have a fight that Friday in Madison Square Garden. Fuck me, there I go again, I thought.

I was eighteen, and as my mother put it, "an adolescent, under the wicked thumb of adolescence," so I guess some mental turmoil was natural. But for me—and no one knew this—it all started in the sixth grade . . .

One day I went to school and learned that a girl had started a "Peter Watt Fan Club." Every girl in the sixth grade joined. I don't know why. I didn't seek it out. It was mass hysteria. Suddenly, girls were groveling for my autograph, my pens, my pencils, my fruit-loop from my shirt and locks of my hair. I tried to live up to what these crazy girls were idolizing. And I did—for a while.

In the eighth grade, I was voted "Most Popular." When you are voted "Most Popular," most people think much more of you than they should, and you convince yourself you're a lot better than you really are.

I don't like to admit it but in my mind, the kids at school were important to me. They became something like family. They replaced my real family which was shattered and destroyed by the Ceffones.

But when I started high school, it all ended. My *school family* grew into new people with new directions and goals. I became lost. I felt like a passing trend—a yo-yo or a Hula-Hoop. A big noise from grammar school who still wants to be heard must find new instruments to play.

WAS—that's a monster of a word.

As I slouched in my chair, I realized that now I never felt comfortable around the other kids. I guess I was the type of guy who never got up when he was knocked down. School was bad and a classroom was worse. I began skipping classes. I'd hop on a bus and escape into New York City—the Bowery. Bums fascinated me. Somehow, I felt like one of them. I was a was. Just like that poor guy my father once told me about—Max Streets.

The corner seat of the back row of Mrs. Simon's class was a good hiding spot, too, the next best thing to the Bowery.

With me were Tommy Crooks and Steve Turner. They were bums hiding, too. Tommy, a slow-reading lip-mover, was a good kid, but he was damaged goods. He let his parents get the best of him. His mom was a slut and his father was the town drunk. Steve's parents were okay, but Steve was crazy and he had green teeth. He once stood up in front of Mr. Brown's remedial math class, dropped his dungarees and yelled, "HOW'S THIS FOR AN IRRATIONAL FRACTION?!" (Ten years later, the Army medics found out he wasn't kidding—he really was crazy. He was diagnosed, and discharged, as a raving paranoid schizophrenic.)

I had a way of attracting crazies. For some reason, I felt comfortable with them. I guess we were all second stringers—all damaged goods.

As Mrs. Simon lectured, I practiced my signature. I wrote with my left hand first, then my right hand. I looked at my first signature. It was neat, straight and disciplined. Another version was a bit messy, but flashy and unique. A third type was awkward and crablike, but powerful. It amazed and disturbed me how, at eighteen, I could have three signatures so different. Everyone else in my senior class was making important decisions like which college to attend and what they were going to be, and I was still deciding how to write my own name. I felt like I was one of my formless, wandering scrawls.

". . . which brings us to the quote," lectured Mrs. Simon, " 'I am cabined, cribbed, confined, bound in to saucy doubts and fears.' Who said this and why?"

I peeked quickly at Mrs. Simon and her tight, severe bun. Her steely eyes darted around the classroom like cold, roving pinballs. Then her icy gaze stopped on the top of my head. I felt her stare in my hair.

"Peter?"

"Yes?"

"Who am I quoting?"

"Shakespeare," I said, not trying to be smart. Nervous giggles and muffled laughter seeped through the room.

"Which character, Mr. Smart-guy?" she asked dryly.

"Well, I think that, uh . . ." I looked at Tom and Steve for help.

"Mick Jagger, Mick Jagger," whispered Steve, smirking.

"Did you read the assignment?" snapped Mrs. Simon, like a rubberband.

"Yes," I lied, "but I haven't gotten that far yet."

"Just say you don't know—don't waste our time with your excuses."

Shame burned inside me. The former grammar school star—Most Popular—bites the dust.

As eager hands waved in the air—the serious students in the first row, mostly—I clenched and unclenched my sweaty toes inside my stinky sneakers.

"That was Macbeth himself," answered Barry Peterman, "upon hearing that Fleance had escaped from the murderer who had killed Banquo."

"Correct," Mrs. Simon said, annointing Barry with a smile.

"Mrs. Simon?" Barry called out from a big fat hole in his face that was his mouth.

"Yes?"

"That was on the very first page," he said smugly. The class laughed loudly. Seething, I was so self-conscious I could feel the liquid on my eyeballs burn. I chewed the inside of my cheek and squirmed in my seat. I didn't like being a dunce, but there wasn't much I could do, except listen to everyone laugh. That was the worst—having a fast-thinking jerk making me look like a fool.

I hated smart kids. They used their minds like boxing gloves. I had the urge to sandwich Barry Peterman's intelligent head between a volume of Shakespeare's collected works and a fat English dictionary and slam them together.

In Mr. Mott's gym class, a lard-ass like Barry was stupid and uncoordinated. Mincing about in his gym shorts with those chubby legs of his, he looked as white and soft as a grub. But I never harassed him. Maybe I should start, I thought. If you show people that you can hurt them, they'll respect you and leave you alone. You've got to show people you're dangerous, otherwise they'll walk all over you. Intelligent kids ate up athletic kids every chance they got—it made them feel more athletic.

Before any more damage could be inflicted, the bell rang, ending class.

"Saved by the bell, tough guy!" joked Tommy.

"You hope Gillio don't fuck you up like fat Barry Peterman!"

blurted crazy Steve. Gillio, I remembered was the Navy fighter.

"Gillio?" asked Tommy, squinting at Steve. "Green! Jamal Green is the guy to beat. The way he punches, he could hospitalize a brick."

I ignored my screwy friends and picked up my books and headed toward the door.

"Gillio, man. Didn't you see how he wasted that dude last week? Whap! One punch!" argued Steve, eyes popping.

"Yeah," said Tommy, "but Green got the Best Fighter of the Night Award."

"A trophy, big shit," said Steve. "Gillio is tougher. Pete, watch out for Gillio; he'll kill ya."

Tommy tugged at my sleeve and advised, "No, Jamal Green, man. He's death."

As I walked out the classroom door, I heard my name called. "Peter!"

I stopped and turned. It was Mrs. Simon.

"Peter, come here please."

I walked to her desk. She was busy shuffling papers.

"Is there some reason why you didn't read your assignment?" she asked without looking up at me. Feeling like a thoroughbred idiot, I said, "No, ma'am."

A small piece of silence hung in the air.

"I didn't want to embarrass you in front of the class, but I wish that you'd start hitting the books instead of people," she said quietly.

I stood watching Mrs. Simon shuffle papers. I knew a teacher could never understand me. I wasn't too smart, strictly second string, and I'd never be quick-witted like fat Barry Peterman. My stammering confidence and intellectual rigor mortis would never enable me to compete with those types. So why try? My *chain* of thought was a *strain* of thought. Teachers would never understand because they were the first-stringers.

"That's all. You can go," she said.

My smelly Cons squeaked as I turned to leave. As I walked out the door, I told myself that I didn't want to be smart. I didn't like first-stringers, the smart types, like my stepfather. They used their intellect like a weapon. I had better things to do with my mind. Dougie, one of the most brilliant boys in our class, hung himself in his basement, and he was the smartest kid I ever knew.

I told myself that it wasn't smart to be smart, and I didn't want to be stupid enough to be smart, like Dougie or fat Barry Peterman or my stepfather. Sports were the only thing in this world that made sense. The flying spiral of a football is a perfectly tossed equation; I could do that. A knockout punch is a perfectly pithy precept; I could do that. A boxing match is a boxer's novel; I could do that, too. I didn't have an articulate mouth, but just as a ballerina has articulate toes, I had articulate fists. And I could compete with my fists. Mrs. Simon could shove it.

Besides, sometimes it's not good to think. That way, you don't realize how bad things really are. Ever since my mother got my brother and me tangled up with the Ceffones, I got into the habit of not thinking. It was my best survival mechanism. If you think too much, you dig too deep and get confused. If I had allowed myself to think how bad the situation was, I would have become so depressed that I'd have ended up like my brother, or I'd have found a rope and ended up like Dougie. Instead, I started boxing. Mrs. Simon could go fuck herself.

As I walked out of the trailer into the freezing cold, I was frowning. I walked through the falling snow. It had gotten warmer, and the snow was more like a thick, slushy rain. It fell limply from the sky like phlegm. I spit out of the side of my mouth and pretended Gillio was watching.

Nonchalantly, I stood beside my locker. I tried to make it appear as if I wasn't waiting, even though I was. I flipped through a *Ring Magazine* to see where they had ranked my favorite fighter, Oscar Bonavena—the Argentinian Wild Bull. Mostly, however, I watched the girls. Secretly I guessed which ones were virgins and which ones weren't. Sometimes I eyed the prettier girls as they pitter-pattered past and imagined what they would look like if they had a big, stiff cock stuck in their mouth.

Also, I never told this before, but sometimes a faintly weird thought would cross my mind—when I'd be talking to a girl, looking at her pretty face, I'd sometimes imagine what she'd look like if I were to punch her in the mouth. I would imagine her carefully arranged hair flying back and her made-up face contorted. Then she wouldn't look so sexy, would she? I never knew why I thought that.

But I didn't think those thoughts with Valerie, my girlfriend. She was the prettiest piece I'd ever known. I'd never seen a girl in *Playboy* or on television more beautiful. The only thing I didn't like was that she smoked cigarettes and popped acid. Other than that, she was perfect.

"Pete! How ya doin', sexy?" she said as she bounced over and brushed beside me. Her long thick black hair trailed down to her thin waist and tickled my arm. She was a junior, a year younger than me.

"I guess you're off to the boxing gym now, huh?" she asked.

"Yeah," I said, looking into her beautiful brown eyes.

"Well, I just wanted to remind you that I haven't seen you in a while."

"Well, you know how it is," I said. "After the Gloves, it'll ease up."

"I miss you," she said softly. She stroked my stomach gently.

"Look, Valerie . . ."

"No," she said, "I miss you. I sort of, *love* you, too."

I looked away.

"I admire you, Pete," she said. "I really admire what you're doing—training hard and sacrificing. Not hanging around, like everyone else, not drinking and not . . . not, you know."

"I know?" I said.

"You know . . . no sex. You're going after something, well, more important."

"Valerie . . ."

"No, I'm proud of you. I'd be scared to death if I had to get into the ring with one of those bozos. I don't know how, or why, you do it but I'll be glad when it's all over."

Me, too, I felt like saying, but didn't.

"I'll be glad when it's all over and we can . . . you know," she said softly. Her eyes twinkled.

"What?"

"You know," she said giggling. She stood on her tiptoes and whispered, "Fuck each other." She looked at me closely. I looked away quickly. If you want to know the truth, I was frightened. I was scared that I'd get stuck there with her, enjoying myself. I couldn't get too comfortable. It was too easy for me to be weak. I had a date with Mudbone Hopkins that I couldn't miss. I didn't want to lapse into the most debilitating state of all—contentment. So I closed my locker and paced down the hall toward my car. Valerie followed.

"A lot of kids are buying tickets to see you fight Friday," she said.

"Oh yeah?" I said.

"Klie is buying tickets and already he's got thirty. He said if it keeps up, he's gonna rent a bus."

"Huh." I had already started preparing for my sparring match with Hopkins. I tried to tune her out. Walking down the hall I recalled a fist fight I had two years ago with a wise-ass named Billy Bickle in this very section of the hall. He was a senior, me a sophomore. Fast thinking, he had the gym teacher believing that I had pinned up a *Hustler* centerfold in the locker room when it was really him. I remember how awful Bickle looked when I got finished with him. I normally go for the face, but this time I went downstairs and cracked two of his ribs—left hooks.

". . . and guess what?" said Valerie.

"Wha . . . ?" I grumbled, thinking about Bickle puking in the hall.

"That's not all," she said excitedly.

I looked at her.

"Bob Hershan spoke with the Madison Square Garden people and they said it was okay if he brings his movie camera and shoots moving pictures of your fight."

I swiveled my neck nervously.

"What's wrong?" she said.

"I don't want to hear that stuff," I said softly. Most Popular was a role that no longer suited me. Now I was a fighter. A fighter who was about to spar with Mudbone Hopkins . . .

FIVE

THE THIRD FIGHT

The Pet Tiger

"IN THE BLUE CORNER—REPRESENTING NEW YORK RECREATION—FROM HARLEM—WITH TWO KNOCKOUTS—JAMAL GREEN!" bellowed the announcer.

From across the ring, I peeked at Green. That was a mistake. One thought sped through the chaos of my mind—was he human?

He had bulging arms and a massive flat chest and the kind of stomach muscles I remembered from comic-book pictures of The Hulk. His black licorice skin glistened with sweat as he swiveled at his waist to loosen up. His long arms reached almost to the floor. He looked like he'd crawled out of the belly of Africa.

"You ain't fightin' *it* till I hear *it* speak," Tom said. "It looks like a fuckin' monkey," he added.

But my confidence was up. I reminded myself that a good physique doesn't make anybody tough. Plus, I was no longer an unknown commodity to myself. I had scored two knockouts, I had trained hard with Mudbone Hopkins (I sported a black eye to prove it), and I felt enough hate coursing through my veins to make me brave.

"I can't believe what these fuckin' guys t'row you," said Tom pulling off my white terrycloth robe with the green shamrock stitched on the back.

"Don't matter," I said softly, conserving energy, "I want him." Green had come here tonight to kick my ass but I was planning to crack his thick skull instead.

"Okay then, dance. Move! Stay away from *it,*" instructed Tom.

During the ref's instructions, we glared at each other from a range of two inches. We were about the same height, five-foot-ten, Green and me. The stench of his breath was sickening, something between a tuna fish sandwich and a fart. I tried not to breathe it in—not that the polluted air of New York's Felt Forum was much better.

His nose was broad and flat, and he had a thick lower lip. He was eyeballing me hard, trying to spot fear in me. I was mentally mauling him, trying to show that I welcomed what was to come. Black guys irritated me royally; they always think you're scared of them because they're black.

His eyes were strong, like chips of steel, and for a split second, even though I hated to, I jerked my eyes away quickly. I glimpsed over Green's shoulder into the crowd.

Right then, I almost fainted. My eyes focused upon Mr. Sgro, my football coach. I hadn't expected him to attend the fight. He was sitting back in his chair, his thick hairy arms crossed, and glaring directly into me—like Green. His football religion was death. Four years of cruel and sadistic football practices, agonizing wind-sprints, inhuman double sessions, heat, sweat and pain swept past me. Quietly, I thanked him and stared back hard at Green.

"Any questions?" asked the referee. "Okay, shake hands and come out at the bell."

Instead of shaking, Green raised his glove, squinted and

pointed at me and sneered, "You owe Allah a death, sucker, and I's gonna do it."

I don't know if I was what you would call afraid, but my heart beat like a bird's, quick and little.

I walked back to my corner.

"Asshole's boxin' you with his mouth," Tom said. "Kill his ass!"

Tiny thumps, like punches, thrummed in my chest. My mouthpiece was snug around my teeth.

Waiting for the bell to ring, half-naked in my corner—wearing green nylon trunks, white wrestling shoes and ten-ounce gloves—I heard the crowd roar as one who sleeps hears.

Green charged at the bell. The smoky air quivered with question marks.

Green, like my first opponent, Joe Burns, was in a big hurry to prove he was tough.

I maneuvered back, just out of reach, waiting for him to throw the first punch—so I could start throwing mine.

I didn't have to wait long. With lefts and rights curving through the air, grunting with each punch, Green hurtled toward me. He didn't waste time with jabs, he threw bombs.

Trying to keep myself out of the hospital, I arched back and danced. I picked off most of his wild shots, but a dangerous and sneaky right hook smacked onto my face. Dancing away, I smiled. Yeah, his punch was hard, but it didn't hurt. I guess, if nothing else, I did have a lot of bone in my skull.

He pursued quickly; he must have thought that he was in there with another knockout victim. I clinched.

"You owe Allah a death, white devil!" he said, grunting, "and I's gonna do it now!" He shoved me away and attacked.

But already I had seen his flaws. He had two. First, although he was a banger, he didn't throw his punches straight. Secondly, he was off balance. So I kept moving and feinted with shoulders and feet to keep him guessing.

As a kid, I had learned about feinting from a gray-covered book my father had bought me. I bet that when I had been reading a book about fighting, Green had been in the streets doing it. In a way, I felt like a studious Barry Peterman.

But what I had learned from that book was working.

I sucked in Green with a few weak, unextended jabs—basic lies—showing how soft they were. Then I stepped in with three long, hard jabs. Splat! Splat! Splat! But I guess he was feinting, too, because, in exchange, he nailed me good.

THUD! This right hand stung. He caught me flush on my jaw. I saw stars, bright pin-pricks of light. Tommy Crooks was right, his punch could hospitalize a brick.

But I made sure I smiled anyway—another lie.

"C'mon, devil, c'mon!" he goaded.

I didn't need to be called a devil to get angry. My mind was frothing. Hate had been spewing out of me since I had pranced from my dressing room. Since that morning, I had been digging into myself to find that delicate personal feeling that was both calm and ferocious, and in the mud of my heart I'd found it. Festering in me was my mother and my stepfather and my family. They generated a potent and poignant and absolute hate.

I loved hate, it was such a good motivation.

Grunting with fury, Green rushed again. He let sail his knock-out punch—the right hook. I ducked, leaned in and countered with a left hook. My full weight, shoulder and hate were behind it. It splattered onto his face. I watched him crumble in pieces—feet, ankles, knees . . . As he fell, quick reflexes and instinct enabled me to drill him with a right uppercut. The punch caught him beneath the chin and bent his head back. He completed his downward crash—trunks, upper body and head.

I ran to the neutral corner and watched the referee count.

ONE . . . TWO . . . THREE.

My heart, pumping wildly, spewed out a joyous hate.

FOUR . . . FIVE . . . SIX . . .

Vaguely, I heard the crowd cheering, but I also heard booing. This puzzled me. I surmised that there were a lot of blacks in the crowd who would be rooting for Green. Also, I wondered what my right uppercut had looked like to the crowd. I suspected that they had mistakenly thought I had hit Green when he was down. I also was concerned that after my last fight, when I fell on the guy, I had gotten a "dirty fighter" reputation.

SEVEN . . . EIGHT . . .

Groggily, Green got up. He looked at me, smiled and—I couldn't believe it—winked.

Some guys are toughest when hurt. They grow teeth, claws and balls. Maybe Green was one.

I attacked with caution.

Hands up, I pawed high and low with two darting jabs to test his coordination. I connected with his stomach but missed his face. He threw a left hook counter. He was a split second slower, but still dangerous.

I studied as I circled. I noticed Green's stance had widened. I suspected that he was hurt and needed extra balance. Too wide a stance might give power, but it takes away speed and efficiency.

It was only when he threw a right and his right leg swung around with it that I was sure he was hurt.

Now was a good time to use the Rockaway.

The Rockaway was a move that I had worked on for countless hours as a kid in my basement. I had learned it from the gray book. Up till then, I used it on shadows and imaginary opponents. Now was for real.

I shuffled forward and feinted with my knees. The feint was to draw Green's jab. From behind my shoulder, I saw Green's jab begin. I dropped my weight to my right foot and moved my body back with his jab. As his jab fell short and returned, I quickly ying-yanged in with my own left and right to his chin.

Smack—SMACK!!

He tumbled to the canvas and his heels flew in the air.

It was beautiful. And the crowd thought so, too, they were yelling their heads off.

Violence is beautiful. Not beautiful in the sense that you condone it, but beautiful because you master fear. You execute and execute well, despite fierce obstacles. Violence is an ironic beauty.

But Green wasn't so beautiful when he got off the canvas at the count of eight. Red blood streamed from his nostrils, down his chin and onto his massive chest. His nose appeared broken and his legs wobbled. In the amateurs, when a fighter looks like Green, they usually stop the fight.

But the bell rang. Dick McCool, the referee, let it continue, to the approval of the crowd.

"Did good, did good!" said Tom pulling my mouthpiece from my lips, "How you feel?"

I nodded my head okay. But I had thrown a lot of punches, and I was breathing hard. In the background, I heard my friends cheering. I felt like I was a high school football team. The worst thing would be to let them down. I knew that I was far ahead, but I also knew that I was a damn asthmatic who got winded easily.

"You're tired," said Tom peering anxiously into my face. He dug into his hip pocked and pulled out a small glass vial.

"Drink," he rasped, holding it to my mouth.

"What . . ."

"Just drink, damn it! Hurry up!"

I drank. It tasted bitter, like bile. But I was so hot, I would have swallowed a pickle.

"Gives energy," said Tom, quickly stuffing the vial back into his pocket with jerky, punch-drunk movements. I didn't give much thought to his mysterious bottle, I had other things to worry about.

"Now listen," he said, his egg-yellow teeth flashing close to my face, "Strategy. I want you to *move*. Then, *stop* movin' and step in quick. Catch him off balance. Move in and out before this guy can set. Don't slug."

I looked at Tom's face—the good side. The bad side stared indifferently upward. Years ago, it had been punched into mush sparring Tony Canzoneri, Barney Ross and Lou Ambers. That's what Tom told me.

"Keep movin'—REPEAT!" he shouted, with damaged vocal cords.

"Keep movin'," I echoed.

"Attack suddenly—REPEAT!"

"Attack suddenly," I repeated.

"No sluggin'—REPEAT!"

"No sluggin'."

In his own way, he was good with words—he kept things simple and bare.

The ten-second buzzer sounded.

As usual, Tom saved his best advice for last. As he bent his old, battered body through the red velvet ropes, he croaked, "Use the left hook."

Jamal Green didn't look so great when he came off his stool for the second round. But I wasn't taking chances. He could be playing possum or could sneak in a lucky punch. I just wanted to take him out quick and go home. Boxing is a savage sport, and when people start punching each other, they bleed. When one of these surly geeks hits you straight on, you feel it good.

As Tom instructed, I looked to throw the left hook.

Everything revolved around my hook. I never was too far from a position in which it could be thrown. I was like Rick Barry, the pro basketball player, who had one special "sweet spot" on the court where his shot was almost guaranteed and every one of his moves had been designed to get to that spot.

Looking at Green from behind my guard, he appeared near finished. I knew that when a fighter has shot his wad, as I hoped Green had, he usually forgets everything but his right hand. Gambling, I stepped closer and stuck out my chin more than usual.

I looked for his right hook.

I was correct! He threw it. Countering, I threw my left hook at the same time.

Mine landed. SPLAT!

Power and fear and anger sped through the muscles of my left arm and bunched into my balled fist. It exploded onto his jawbone. The force distorted his face, and his body dropped clean away. His head bounced on the canvas.

His face, when it finally turned up at the count of six, looked peaceful. His fishlike, glassy eyes stared blankly up at the ring lights as if he were watching television.

The crowd burst into a roar, excited howls and gleeful cackles. I guess they liked the way in which Green dropped—it was pleasantly ugly and gently cruel. I assume that the many psychologically troubled fight fans in the Felt, the screaming ones with hate etched across their faces, had been satisfied.

And so were my friends.

I pranced down the aisle after having scored my third knockout in three fights. Anonymous fans and cheering high school friends were jumping up and down, like popcorn, all around me.

I remembered Mrs. Simon stating once in English class that "Plays purify the morals." That might be true, but boxing did something better—it disinfected my soul.

I felt strangely cleansed and light.

I felt no hate. Within me was an inner glow, something, I imagined, like what a Catholic feels like after confession.

There was no hate. Boxing helps suck up emotional mire. It's something like ironing wrinkles from a shirt.

This stutterer, bedwetter, thumbsucker, asthmatic, former Most Popular wasn't feeling like a stutterer, bedwetter, thumbsucker, asthmatic, former Most Popular anymore. He felt clean and elated.

Like a healthy person.

I had trained hard, I had won and I hadn't let down my friends. I was enjoying this morsel of happiness as Valerie kissed my cheek and friends patted my back. I felt like I was someone I used to know—myself.

I was eating it up until a black woman from the crowd raced up to me and shouted, "Fuck you, ya fuckin' devil!" Then she gobbed in my face.

A man peeked inside our dressing room door. "I'm looking for Pete Watt."

"I'm Watt," croaked Tom.

As the man entered, I saw clutched in his hand a spiraled notebook and a yellow pencil; a "PRESS" card was pinned to his white shirt.

"I'm looking for the fighter who just knocked out Green."

"What you like to know?" asked Tom.

"Well, I want to speak with your boy."

"I talk for him," said Tom. "My fighters ain't too good at talking." He inserted a small Jersey City pause and added, "If they could talk good, they wouldn't be fighters, would they?"

The reporter leaned his shoulder against the wall and asked, "Mind if I start?" Judging by his sour expression, it didn't look like he enjoyed his job much.

"Ask away, mister. We got all the time in the world," said Tom.

"Well, if you wanna know the truth," he said, "I'm going to the track so I don't think this'll take too long."

Tom made a funny face behind the reporter's back.

"Preparing for a fight," asked the reporter, "what type of roadwork you do?"

"My pet tiger here runs three miles a day," answered Tom.

"Pet tiger?" the reporter said, laughing.

"Colorful, ain't it?" asked Tom proudly.

"Five days a week," I said, trying to speed things up.

"Does your pet tiger run sprints, too?" the reporter asked.

"Twenty fifteen-yard wind-sprints—telephone poles," I said quickly.

"I only wanted fifteen," croaked Tom.

"I've been up to twenty, sometimes twenty-five," I said.

Sprints, I found, were the best exercise to counteract asthma.

Tom shrugged. The reporter continued.

"When do you spar?"

"Five days a week," offered Tom, "five to eight three-minute rounds, that's enough."

"What's your best fighting weight?"

"Sixty-three," said Tom.

"No problem making weight?"

"No," I said, "I lose three to five pounds each workout."

"How long is a workout?"

"Usually forty-five minutes. Heavy bag, light bag, exercises, sparring . . ."

"In and out quick," added Tom.

"Just like here," quipped the reporter, busily jotting notes.

"Okay, Pete, what is your best punch?" asked the reporter, flipping back a slice of paper in his notebook.

"You mean," croaked Tom, "what's his best *weapon.*"

"Okay, weapon . . . left hook?"

"Anger—that's his best weapon," Tom said. "It's his best emotion. He ain't too good with others."

"Anger?" asked the reporter, looking up.

"That's it, anger. He's boiling inside. I recognize it 'cause I was the same myself when I fought. But Pete here," said Tom patting my back, "he's always been that way, since he came into my gym. He can't help it. That's his nature."

The reporter looked at me funny. "What are you angry at, son?"

Before I could say None of your fuckin' business, Tom chuckled.

"Don't matter what he's angry at," said Tom. "He keeps it tied in a knot and hangs on to it. That's a sign of a good fighter. He don't tell nobody nothin'. His anger is like water clingin' to the tilted rim of a glass. He keeps it all inside until he spills it into the ring."

"Onto someone's face, right?" asked the reporter.

"Right," Tom said, laughing.

The reporter looked at us as if we smelled rotten. "Pussycat outside of the ring, tiger inside, right?" he asked snidely.

"You got it!" said Tom proudly. "Peter here is an ice-cold, self-centered, mean-spirited, arrogant kid with a beautiful left hook. You write *that.*"

"Beautiful," said the reporter.

"That's right, it *is* beautiful, dickhead!" shot Tom, pouncing on his attitude. "A fighter is a pure artist—don't sit there with your fat belly and your skinny pencil and say he ain't. A fighter, like Pete here, is his own canvas and brush. He expresses himself that way. A fighter's got his own language—boxin'. Fightin' is a poor guy's art. I should know, I was a fighter myself. I kicked Tony Canzoneri's ass more than once, ya know."

"I really don't think I care to hear about Tony Canzoneri," said the reporter tiredly. "I simply want two columns about the boy."

"Hell!" shot Tom, reddening. "You're gonna hear about Canzoneri 'cause I'm teachin' this kid what Canzoneri taught me and what Charley Burley taught him and what Jack Dempsey taught him, Bearcat Wright taught him, Sam Langford, Peter Jackson, all the way down the line to Molineaux!"

"All I want is two columns, pal," muttered the reporter. "Like I said, I don't even want to be here."

"Look at him," ordered Tom, pointing to me. "What you're lookin' at is a piece of boxin' evolution. Too bad you can't appreciate."

The reporter must have found this interesting, he began scrawling notes.

"When this kid wants to hook your jaw, he does. When he wants to hook your belly, he does. When he wants to hook your balls, he does. If he wants to slug with a slugger or box with a boxer, he'll do it. He don't make mistakes 'cause he's gettin' my education." Tom sat back triumphantly.

"Too bad his education doesn't include defense," said the reporter dryly.

"What you mean?"

"His defense has holes in it."

"Your nose has holes in it!" spat Tom.

The reporter chuckled. "If I recall correctly, he got slammed pretty hard in the first. For a moment, I thought he was going down."

"Listen," said Tom, "Green is a good fighter. He's allowed to land a few good licks."

"How about that black eye?" asked the reporter, pointing to my face. "That speaks for itself. He didn't get that eating cupcakes, did he?"

"Sparrin' Mudbone Hopkins. Ever hear of him?"

"Can't say I have."

"Didn't think so," croaked Tom.

"Nevertheless, when your pet tiger here climbs into the ring with some of the other guys . . ." he looked down at his pad and flipped some pages, "Let's see, who's left . . . Gillio, Jones, Capobianco, Valero, Griffith, Centano and Roundtree. Every one of those kids can punch and your fighter—if he's to survive—needs better defense."

Tom waved his hand in the air. "My fighter's method of defense is such that he don't need none."

"Like Chuck Wepner?"

"You know Chuck?" asked Tom brightly.

"Everyone knows the Bayonne Bleeder."

"Yeah, Chuck's got that god-awful thin skin," said Tom touching his eyebrows.

"You're Chuck's trainer, too, aren't you?" inquired the reporter.

"Ain't got nothin' to do with anything," said Tom, reddening at the reporter's insinuation.

The reporter smiled. "Okay, last question. I'd like the kid to answer, if that's okay with you."

"Make it quick," said Tom.

The reporter looked at me squarely. "I've always wanted to know *why* people box. Why do you box?"

I thought for a minute, but I couldn't think of any good reasons—reasons I would want published.

"Well, I don't know," I stammered, ". . . I just . . ."

"What do you get out of it?"

I honestly couldn't come up with an answer.

"If you gotta know," interrupted Tom, "it's because the boy is sick, that's why. Anybody who fights in a ring's gotta be crazy. Look at him, he's fuckin' cockeyed!"

The reporter shook his head and flipped his book shut.

"Okay, I think I got my story. Thanks, it's been a treat." Halfway out the door, he turned. "I almost forgot." He looked at me, "Where do you attend school, son?"

"Hudson High, in Jersey City, why?" intervened Tom quickly.

"I asked your pet tiger, not you," snapped the reporter.

"Hudson High," I echoed.

"That's strange," said the reporter, toying with his pencil. "All your friends here tonight attend Old Tappan." He looked at me, then Tom, and smiled. "Why's that?"

"He transferred schools, that's why," offered Tom. "He's livin' with me now."

"You realize that he's ineligible to continue this tournament if the officials learn that he's living in Old Tappan, don't you?"

"Don't cause trouble. He's been livin' with me two years," lied Tom.

"Is that so?"

"I told ya, he's crazy—he don't get along with his parents."

The reporter quickly jotted something onto his pad, looked up and said, "Okay, we'll see about that." He walked briskly out the door.

"Don't worry," said Tom, trying to hide his concern. "You're sellin' too many tickets for them to t'row you out now." Then he began chewing a fingernail.

The thought of getting disqualified made me inwardly exuberant, but outwardly nauseous. I walked into the bathroom to take a leak. Next to the urinal, written on the white wall was:

WHITEY EATS SHIT
—Muhammed Ali

(Written below it was:)
ALI FARTS DUST
—Jerry Quarry

I looked at my piss squirt into the white porcelain bowl; it was light brown. I thought, then, about Tom's vial.

SIX

THE FAMILY

Harmonizing

After the Green fight, I was still secretly twisting napkins into tight knots in my lap beneath the dinner table at home. I had always sensed that they were the captors and I was the captive. But by then, I had found one effective way of surviving the Ceffones—I held everything in. I had to appear as if I was harmonizing with them, so, every now and then, to show them I was, I'd smile.

After ten shitty years with those assholes, I'd learned that if I couldn't shut them up, I could at least shut them out: Rodney, Lance, Raquel, Stacie, my mother and most important, the old man. It amazed me how I could live with people for twenty-four hours a day, for ten years, and still not know them. The Ceffones, if you let them, could reach up and grab you by the throat and bring you down.

It didn't take me long to discover that Mr. Ceffone had a mind like a sharp knife. He constantly whittled us down thinner and thinner, honing and perfecting his logic and constitutional law on us. We were unwilling sparring partners. These onslaughts were not intended to educate, only massacre. Most of the time, we just sat with bowed heads, staring at the floor.

I remember one evening two months before the Gloves started. My stepfather was sitting on a couch next to the television set. The pressure of his potbelly brought out the shape of his cock on his thigh. He looked up from a stack of legal documents on his lap to watch the six o'clock news. A helmeted cop from the Washington, D.C., Police Department was slamming a nightstick into the ear of a young demonstrator at a Nixon rally. My stepfather tapped cigar ashes into his coffee cup and said, "Damn hippies."

"The cop shouldn't be hitting him like that," I uncharacteristically volunteered.

"And why not, may I ask?" asked my stepfather, looking at me with an abusive stare.

"Because that kid has freedom of speech."

"That kid," said my stepfather, jutting out his forefinger, "should be thrown in jail."

"How about his freedom of speech?" I asked.

"There should be no freedom of speech unless you earn it."

"The Constitution says . . ."

"The Constitution is wrong," he interrupted. "And it's only a matter of time before it's changed. America is a great country, not because of freedom of speech—don't kid yourself. America is a great country because it's flexible. We can, and will, correct things if necessary."

I knew that this match-up, he and I, was like the demonstrator and the cop with his nightstick. I should have sat back and blended in with the walls and bookcases, but I gave it one last shot. "Still," I insisted, "that cop . . ."

"Policeman to you."

"Policeman. That policeman still shouldn't be clubbing him."

He laughed. "For a somewhat intelligent boy, you can be very dumb sometimes. What you're saying is completely unrealistic. Do you think that when I'm trying a case in court I'd get any respect if I were soft?" He narrowed his eyes and shook his head.

"Don't kid yourself. People respect strength and strength only. Read between the lines. The unwritten law is 'Might Makes Right.' "

"Seems to me," I said, unraveling a thin, feeble voice, "that that kid wasn't doing anything illegal and . . ."

"That kid," he interrupted, "was depriving President Nixon of *his* right of speech! What makes you think that that punk's rights are more important than the president of the United States?"

Near defeat, I shook my head and said in a crumbling voice, "I just feel it was wrong to treat him like that."

"What's wrong to you might be right to me. Sometimes truth is subjective, like a matter of taste. And let me remind you, pal, unless you have a job and are on your own, there'll be no freedom of speech around here, either. You have any problems with that?"

I shook my head.

"Excuse me?" jabbed my stepfather.

"No, sir," I said, trying to get into my voice some of the respect I knew he expected me to feel.

The discussion was over, but my stepfather kept going. As he crossed his legs, I noticed his shoes. They were probably Italian. Made from some soft, unborn calf.

"You can think what you want, but don't ever let me catch you protesting. I feed you. I clothe you. And I'm the one responsible. I'm your government. The only free speech you have is what I allow you to have. Am I understood?"

"Yes, sir." And fuck you and the horse you rode in on, I thought.

He settled back to his legal papers with satisfaction and sucked his tooth.

Really, I think he was disappointed that I wouldn't give him a battle. Maybe some day, I thought.

I walked down to the basement. The basement, where no one else went, was the best place in the entire house. It seemed like a human being sometimes, except it was much better because you could trust it. I could be alone down there and talk to myself and lose myself in punching. I made the house, beyond the basement, a vast gray cloud where nobody else existed.

I had a game I played. I punched rolled-up socks against the walls and pretended I was fighting classmates or heavyweight contenders. When the socks unraveled, it was a knockout. I also punched my "speed bag"—a metal coat hanger that I had bent into the shape of a small bag which hung from an exposed pipe on the ceiling. I went crazy punching. The rhythm of hitting the "bag" made me forget everything.

These were my new playmates—rolled-up socks and a metal coat hanger.

I was too old for Sticko, the Indian.

Down there in the secrecy of the basement, I battered tough Jack Dempsey against the cement wall, I battered black Jack Johnson against a closed door, and I battered a fat Barry Peterman until they all unraveled onto the floor. I bent down, picked them up, and rolled them up again for my next battle. While doing so, I thought about my father. I recalled that strange day six years ago when he picked me up in his car . . .

My father drove into the Ceffone driveway with his white Valiant and honked his horn. It was visitation weekend and, as I ran to his car, I was the happiest twelve-year-old kid in the whole world. I opened the car door and hopped in.

"How's my lad?" Dad said, hugging me.

"Great! But how come you asked me to wear my suit today?" I said, unloosening my necktie.

"We're doing an especially good deed today."

"Ah, we're not going to the synagogue, are we?" I said.

"No," said Dad driving away from the Ceffone mental institution, "we're visiting someone."

"Who?"

"Max Streets," he said.

"Who's Max Streets?"

My father looked surprised. "You never heard of Max Streets?"

"No."

"Well," said my father, suddenly serious, "he was a bloke I used to know. Strange case. He probably could have been a very fine prizefighter . . . but something happened to him."

"What?" I asked.

"I don't know. I don't think anyone knows."

"Where does he live?" I asked, as the refreshing wind from outside the window blew into my face and hair.

"I don't know," said my father. "I don't think the poor fellow has got a home."

"So where will we meet him?"

"The Bronx," said Dad, steering ahead smoothly.

"What's he doing in the Bronx?"

My father looked over at me. "He's lying in a hospital bed."

"Oh," I said, stunned.

"What you see today," he said, "I hope you never forget." He drove on quietly.

"Is he going to die?" I asked.

"Probably," he said, softly. "We all do eventually."

"Soon?" I asked.

"Maybe," he said, turning the car onto the parkway. "I just want us to pay our respects."

"How do you know Max?"

Dad sighed deeply. "That's a story."

"Tell me."

"Are you sure you want to hear it?"

"Yes."

"It's not pleasant," he warned.

"Tell me."

He thought for a long time and then began.

"When I was younger, my first job in America was an assistant music editor for a magazine here in New York. I'd usually eat lunch at a place called Katz's cafeteria. And each day when I entered the cafeteria I'd immediately see this guy. He sat in the corner, despondent, head lowered. He was like a lonely black cloud waiting for the rain. It was Max Streets, a bloke who once had a string of twenty-one knockouts. He had fought in all the New York City fight clubs: St. Nick's, Broadway, Ridgewood and the old Garden. Everyone knew that he was once Gorilla Jones's sparring partner but was let go because he had knocked Jones flat with one left hook."

"Wow!" I said.

"I judged Max then to be in his middle thirties. He was tall but stooped. He wore a tattered gray coat, and a pink scarf was knotted around his neck. You'd never know that he was a fighter except for the way his face was.

"I remember one day walking to the counter, ordering my lunch—a blintze and black coffee—and sitting down facing him. I wouldn't say Max was a derelict, but he was awful close to being one. I remember his skin was dirty like a potato's, and he looked thin as poverty. He was nibbling at something in a sandwich; dirt was beneath his fingernails. Dangling from his wrist I noticed a hospital tag."

"What happened to him?" I asked.

"I don't know. He was such a good fighter," said my father. He looked over at me with my little cue-ball head. "I had once been a fighter, too, you know, an amateur. I had a few fights back in England. But after I broke my nose for the second time my mum asked me to stop. So I stopped." My father smiled. "That's when I started hitting piano keys instead of people."

"You were a good fighter, weren't you, Dad?"

"Never mind that, son. Today, when you look at Max's lopsided face, you will know that you can't play with violence."

I listened as my father continued his story.

"I asked him, 'You're Max Streets, aren't you?' He looked up at me. His face, rough and yellow, resembled a large, callous pickle. 'I've seen you fight,' I said. Suddenly, a massive dose of anguish contorted his face. 'I've seen you fight at St. Nick's. You knocked out Abey Goldstein,' I said. Max averted his eyes.

"It was like I could see memories breathing within his heart.

Suddenly I felt guilty for having entered into his anonymous shadow and having embarrassed him. 'Well,' I stumbled, 'you were a good fighter.' Max looked at me and began to scribble a sentence with his tongue on the roof of his mouth. I could see inarticulation immobilized him. Max, like many good fighters, funneled his thoughts through fists, not mouths. 'You were a *real* good fighter,' I repeated. Max leaned closer. 'I am what I am,' he whispered to me."

"What did he mean?" I asked my father.

Dad shrugged. "I'm not sure. I'm just not sure," he said, thinking.

"A few years passed and I stopped eating at Katz's cafeteria. I was promoted to full music critic at the uptown office. I had forgotten about Max Streets. I didn't even know if he was still alive. Then, one day while browsing through the newspaper, I read a boxing ad. It announced that the middleweight slugger, Tony Bello, was fighting Max Streets in Madison Square Garden. The winner was guaranteed a shot at the middleweight title. Amazing! Was this the same Max Streets? Was this the same poor bloke who was seeking refuge in shadows?"

"Was it, was it?"

My father smiled. "Well, that Friday, I walked to Madison Square Garden and bought a five-dollar ticket to find out. Sitting in the audience, I watched the main-event fighters as they entered. Bello, a Chicago fighter, was first. He was so hairy, he looked as though he was growing a beard on his arms and shoulder blades."

"Ha!" I laughed.

"Then Max entered. It *was* him. He looked fresh and youthful. He bounced up and down wearing a handsome green satin robe with white trim. As his trainer undraped him, Max loomed lean and muscled. The change was astounding. He was no longer the corroded creature sitting in a cafeteria wearing an attitude of death."

"Wow!" I chimed.

"The bell rang. Max came out fast, pawing jabs, sidestepping, countering. Max made Bello lunge and lurch wildly. I smiled. Whatever it was, boxing had resuscitated Max Streets."

"Did he win?" I asked.

"Well," said Dad, "in the sixth, Max decked Bello. On the canvas, with his hairy shoulder blades, he resembled a rug. At the count of nine, Bello stood up, but from the way he looked, it was not a good idea. Seconds later, Bello was a very bloody rug. Max knocked him cold."

"Wow!"

"I used my press pass to enter Max's dressing room after the knockout. Max was perched on a rubbing table talking to reporters. You know, Peter," said my father looking over at me with his big warm smile, "one is rarely granted the opportunity to witness a man's metamorphosis. To me, Max proved the strength and beauty of the human spirit. He had wasted years as a bloody derelict, and now he was on the brink of a world's title. Max had flowered!"

I smiled as I watched my father's enthusiasm bloom. I liked when he smiled. The smile, however, was short-lived. He darkened.

"I listened to Max speak; sweat dripped from his face. I learned that his life was a tough one. He grew up in poverty on the Lower East Side of Manhattan. His grandparents had raised him. But mostly Max spoke about swimming and fishing around the docks, as a kid, near his home. His father was a drunkard, and Max never knew his mother. She had joined a religious order and devoted her life to helping poverty-stricken children in Mexico.

" 'But it don't bother me none,' said Max, shrugging.

" 'It doesn't bother you that you never knew your own mother?' inquired a reporter.

" 'She, I guess, had a higher purpose,' said Max, rubbing his nose.

" 'What're your chances of beating the champ?' asked another reporter, getting down to business.

"Max shrugged again.

" 'He says he's gonna lick you in the first.'

" 'Don't bother me none,' repeated Max, shrugging.

" 'He says youse a bum,' quipped someone from the crowd.

"Max glanced around the room, and I swear there was a flicker of recognition in his eyes when he spotted me.

" 'He says youse a bum!' repeated the voice.

" 'I *ain't* a bum!' shouted Max. 'I proved that tonight, didn't I?' He rubbed his nose.

" 'How you gonna fight him?' asked a reporter. 'Gonna change anything? Style? Strategy?'

"Max shook his head. 'I am what I am,' he said. Then he slid off the rubbing table and disappeared into the locker room."

My father looked over at me. "And that was that, lad. That was the last time I've seen him."

"Why?" I asked. "What happened to him?"

"Well, I'll tell you. A few months passed, and the newspapers reported that Max was being replaced by another middleweight. It was a mystery. It seems that Max had skipped town, but no one actually knew what had happened. He vanished."

"Why?" I asked.

"Your guess, Peter, is as good as mine." My father drove on quietly.

"That's the end of the story?" I asked.

"No, there's more," said Dad. "A few years passed, and the world, and I, forgot about Max Streets. Then, one Saturday, in the middle of winter, I took a cab to my former office downtown. I wasn't working at the magazine any longer. By then, I had started writing my own songs. But since I was in the area, I decided it would be nice to eat lunch at the old Katz's cafeteria. The neighborhood looked even worse. On the curb, I watched an alcoholic coughing and hacking hard; I was certain his liver was going to come out of his mouth."

"Yuck."

"I pushed through the revolving door into the cafeteria. Inside, the warm odors of corned beef, chicken soup and knishes welcomed me. But suddenly my heart dropped onto the floor. I saw something I could not believe. In the corner of the room sat Max Streets. His hair was disheveled, and his sunken eyes stared blankly at the wall. He was yellow and emaciated, and he was still wearing the same gray tattered overcoat. He slowly sipped milk from a small carton."

I was getting frightened of this Max Streets. I didn't want to visit him so much anymore. My father continued his story.

"The cafeteria was crowded, so with a blintze and a coffee balanced on my tray, I approached him.

" 'Excuse me,' I said.

" 'What you want?' asked Max without looking up.

" 'Mind if I sit down?'

" 'It don't bother me none,' he said.

"I sat down. Out of the corner of my eye I watched him sip milk. I wanted to reach out and talk but I remembered how I'd embarrassed him years ago. Had he remembered me? Why had he returned? What caused his slide into self-destruction? I've always wondered. I thought about his mother and his drunkard father. Who was to blame? Well, I gulped back my curiosity and, after I had finished my meal, I stood to leave.

" 'Excuse me, mister,' Max said to me.

"I looked down at his cadaverous face.

" 'You wouldn't have a spare quarter, would you?' "

"So what did you do?" I asked my father.

My father looked over at me and shrugged. "I gave him a dollar."

By this time, I *definitely* did not want to meet Max. But we were already close to the hospital. Dad was looking for a parking spot.

"Well, lad," said my father seriously. "Why do you suppose Max ended up the way he did?"

"I don't know," I said.

He frowned with thought and said, "Neither do I. Neither do I."

We drove on quietly.

"That's a sad story, Dad," I said.

"Yes, it is. But it didn't have to be—that's the point."

"And scary, too," I added.

"Well, what's scary, Peter, is that it's not over yet," he said, slowing the car into a parking spot. "Yesterday, I found a small article on the bottom of the sports page." He handed me a newspaper clipping from his pocket. "Here, you can read it," he said. It read:

> Max Streets, a former boxer, was found meandering dazed and half-naked in lower Manhattan about a mile from the neighborhood where he grew up. Streets was discovered near a deserted area around the docks about 1:00 A.M. He was clad only in undershorts and shoes. A gray overcoat was found draped over a nearby fire hydrant. In it, police found five hundred dollars, articles on his boxing background, and photos of him posing with stars such as David Niven, Bob Hope and Anthony Quinn.
>
> "The answers he'd give you would be polite but they would be gibberish," said Policeman Regino. Streets, apparently senile, was taken to Vets Hospital psychiatric ward.

"Dad," I said nervously, "I don't want to see Max." I was scared, and that's a fact.

When we walked into the hospital, the receptionist told us that Mr. Streets was resting in a double room on the third floor.

Dad bought fifteen dollars' worth of red roses. "He probably has a lot of flowers already," said Dad, "but let's bring them to him anyway."

When we reached Max's room, we knocked on the door and entered. There was a man curled up into a fetal position. He was sucking his thumb. It was Max.

A nurse walked in and stood beside us. "Are you a friend?" she asked.

"Yes, in a way," said Dad. "How is he?"

"All right, I suppose," she said. "He's a gentle one," she added.

"Oh?" said Dad.

"Yes," she said softly. "He likes us to rock him. He calls me 'Mama.' "

Dad grimaced.

The nurse shrugged. "He's like a lot of the other poor street vagrants we get in here."

I looked at Max and was a little terrified. He was sucking his thumb, and his vacant eyes stared into space.

"He was a fine boxer once," said my father.

"Well, that explains his face," said the nurse.

My father gazed down at Max and murmured, "People forget, Max. People forget."

Before we left, Dad bent over and showed Max his flowers. A smile appeared beneath Max's crushed nose. His eyes moistened. He tried to lift himself but couldn't; he tried to speak, but couldn't. Nevertheless, I read his lips—he was trying to say "Beautiful." And they were, but I noticed with an inner wince, that they were the only ones in his room . . .

Dad pressed the "DOWN" button on the elevator. He was quiet. Very quiet. As we waited, I thought about a healthy Max Streets knocking out a hairy Tony Bello in the sixth. I realized that, if Max had died in the ring that night, he would have died a hero, a martyr. But, as it was, he'd die lying between two white Sanforized sheets in a hospital bed. A pug. A lousy forgotten pug with a tag dangling around his wrist. Somehow, it didn't seem right. Or fair.

"I'm sorry, Dad," I said, looking up at him. I was proud of myself—I wasn't frightened of Max anymore. But when I looked into my father's face, I saw a worry line carved into his forehead. And in his eyes I saw fear.

As we walked back to the car, Dad remained quiet. Perhaps he was thinking about his own career. I knew that he, too, was now somewhat of a Max Streets. Or maybe Dad was thinking about his own father—a man he never really knew.

As he drove home my dad said exactly four words. "People forget. People forget."

Down there in the secrecy of the basement I sat quietly; harmonizing with the silence around me. The balled-up socks lay softly in my lap. I thought about my father. I was proud of him. He was strong enough to do something sissyish—give a guy flowers. He didn't even really know him. I didn't understand, and I still don't know why, but he did. It was decent.

Ceffone would never have done it in a million years. Because he was a hard-ass weakling.

I stood up to punch Jack Dempsey again, but then sat down. I saw Max lying there in the hospital bed sucking his thick meaty thumb. I saw Dad's worry line carved into his forehead.

I saw me.

SEVEN

THE GYM

The Screaming Dream

Brandy's Gymnasium in Jersey City is a stink, a thudding noise, a quality of strength, a pit, a moan, a light, a dream, a poem. It is a frowzy old place where the white chipped walls suffer from psoriasis. Zoological smells and flabby brown odors waft through the air. It is not a clean gym, and one should not go barefoot, especially while showering.

I entered Brandy's Gym two days after knocking out Green. The one-day rest was great, but now it was back to work.

When I entered the gym door, it was 4:30 in the afternoon, and the gym was packed, as usual.

Sweaty fighters were panting as they thumped and thwacked heavy bags; small, dark men were masturbating their egos as they shadowboxed into dirty mirrors; a bald lady—Prince Lola—grunted while she sparred. Everyone seemed rabid.

At the round's end, Sugar Parker, a stodgy middleweight, but once a promising welterweight with a 43–0 record, let loose a spine-tingling primal scream.

That was Brandy's Gym.

Taped to the dressing room door was a photo of New Jersey Heavyweight Randy Neumann and a yellow fight poster advertising:

JOSE GONZALES VS. "BAD" BENNIE BRISCOE
(N.Y.C.)   (Philadelphia)

As I opened the door, I thought to myself that boxing is the only profession, besides my stepfather's of lawyering, in which hostility is a virtue.

When I entered the locker room to undress, I remembered my first time in Brandy's. I was seventeen . . .

It was in July—the summer between my junior and senior years and I had convinced myself, finally, that I was ready for the challenge.

I had learned of Brandy's from reading an article on Chuck Wepner in *Ring Magazine*. The gym was located twenty miles from my house and was easy to find—10 Deacon Street.

I remember avoiding the jagged edges of broken whiskey bottles as I carefully parked my black '67 Pontiac next to the curb. Palms sweating, I clutched my duffle bag and nervously walked up the rickety wooden staircase.

Atop was a pool hall. Hoods—the stupid and scrawny type—hung out there. Most of these punks were wearing ripped t-shirts and had rotten teeth. They appeared to be on downers and incapable of hurting anyone, except, maybe, with a knife.

In the back room was the gym. Nervously, I entered. Sitting on a wooden bench, reading the sports section of the *Jersey City Journal* was Tom Brandy. He looked exactly like his picture in *Ring Magazine*.

"Hi. Mr. Brandy?"

"Yeah?" he croaked.

"Hi. My name's P-Peter Watt, and I'd like to enter, ah, join, your club here," I stammered.

"You a fighter?" he asked. His voice was a bit garbled and thick.

"A couple of street fights, that's it," I said. I wanted to appear tough but not too tough. Purposely, I didn't reveal any information about my two hundred street fights. I didn't want him to expect too much from me. Besides, I didn't really feel much tougher than those punks playing pool.

"Where you from?" he asked.

"Rockleigh."

"Where the hell's that?"

"About fifteen miles north of George Washington Bridge, next to Norwood."

"Oh, a rich kid, huh?"

I shrugged. "Not really."

"A guy like you, why the hell you want to be a fighter?" he asked, grinning.

Again I shrugged. "I don't know, just do."

Tom flipped his newspaper shut. He looked up at me and narrowed his eyes. He stood slowly and his knee joints made two dry cracks.

"Let's see," he said, scanning me up and down like a butcher examining a slab of beef. "You about seventy pounds?"

"One hundred and sixty-five," I replied.

"Huh, middleweight," he sniffed.

I nodded.

"Play sports?"

"Football and baseball—varsity," I said.

Tom eyed me closely. "So you like sports?"

"I guess."

"And you like to play sports, right?" he asked.

"Yeah."

"Well, boxin' ain't a sport, kid."

I looked at him.

"You play football—right?"

"Uh-huh."

"And you play baseball—right?"

"Yeah."

"Well, you don't play boxing!" he said. "If I was to say anything, I'd say boxin' is an art—it ain't no sport." Tom walked past me and opened a window. "So, if you came to play, boy, there's the door."

"I came to fight," I said firmly.

Tom turned and looked at me. "Why?"

"I want to win the New York Golden Gloves, that's why," I said.

"But why?"

"I-I-I just do," I stammered.

"A coupla street fights and now you think you're tough, huh?" I shrugged.

"What you say your name was?" he asked, looking me up and down.

"P-P-Pete Watt."

"Okay, P-P-Pete Watt," he chuckled, "I'll give ya your chance. I'll let you spar some o' my fighters. We'll get you in there, see how you look. If you're no good, you'll know, 'cause I'll tell ya. Then I'll kick you out."

"Okay," I said.

"And I want you to understand something else. It'll be hard. Brandy's Gym in Jersey City is a whole different planet from Rockleigh's country clubs, in case you ain't noticed yet."

"Thanks," I said.

"As far as I'm concerned, it's better to box and *lose* than play tennis and *win*," he spat.

I nodded in agreement.

"Yeah, I'll take ya on," he said, grinning. "We'll see what you got. And let me tell you something else. I'm the best damn trainer you'll ever find in this whole damn hemisphere! If anybody can make you a fighter, Mr. White Rich Boy, it'll be me."

In the gym the following day, I was loosening up, stretching the hamstrings with a football exercise, when Tom said, "Boy, I want to show you something." I followed him as he shuffled toward the elevated ring. He pointed through the frayed ropes (that were patched together with silvery electrical tape) at the canvas.

"See that?" he croaked.

I looked but saw nothing. "See what?" I asked.

"Look on the canvas."

I looked closer and saw a large dried bloodstain.

"That shit came outta the nose of Sonny Liston!" He pointed toward another brown splotch in the corner.

"See that?" he said.

"Yeah."

"Emile Griffith." He motioned towards more brown marks. "Hurricane Carter . . . Jimmy Dupree . . . Wepner . . . Miguel Barahona . . . Frankie DePaula . . ." Then he reached into the ring and touched, almost petted, a large plop of dried blood.

"And this one, believe it or not, came out of The Rock's nose!"

"The Rock?" I asked.

"Marciano! He trained here for, I think, LaStarza in the old Garden."

I didn't know if he was putting me on or what.

"You think you can handle this place, boy?" croaked Tom. "There's no sense gettin' your brains scrambled for nothin', is there?"

"I can handle it," I said, throwing soft punches in the air. I was feeling optimistic because I didn't know any better.

"You gotta want it and want it bad," he said.

"I want it."

"You gotta *taste* it."

I nodded my head.

"A lotta new fish come in here sounding just like you. They read books or see movies, and all of a sudden, they wanna be fighters, but the first time they're roughed up, they forget to come back." He turned and pointed to Marciano's brown plop stain and said, "You gotta have that dream screamin' inside you, and you gotta do whatever it takes to get it."

I didn't know a fucking thing about this screaming dream that he spoke about, but I did have one wild hair up my ass. I *had* to fight, not because I wanted to, but because I *had* to.

It was all stuffed platitudes—what Tom had said. I had heard the same stale speech from my football coach about "tasting it." With him, however, it was football. "FOOTBALL IS YOUR LIFE! WHEN YOU PLAY FOOTBALL FOR ME, YOU GOTTA EAT WITH A FOOTBALL, SLEEP WITH A FOOTBALL AND SHIT WITH A FOOTBALL . . ."

Coaches and trainers pissed me off. They always tried to scare and test you with their challenge shit. And they always treated a guy like dirt, hoping he'd do something great. It was always the same.

And I didn't know what Tom was talking about "boxing being art," either. If an audience wanted art, they'd go to a museum, not a prize fight. To me, boxing wasn't art; it was something halfway between religion and war.

I looked at Tom and gritted my teeth. This new fish, I thought, will show you a fucking scream that'll pop your eardrums . . .

After the Green fight, I walked into the gym locker room. Sitting nude, except for his white socks, was Otho Tyson, a slender black welterweight from Paterson. Otho was pro and worked as a garbage man on the side. He had the quickest reflexes in the entire gym. He could hit a speed bag quicker with one hand than anyone could with two. Unfortunately, one evening in North Bergen Arena, his reflexes weren't quick enough and his two front teeth were punched out.

Otho was sitting in a metal chair flicking dirt from his navel. He spoke with Rodell Dupree—describing a girl he'd once dated.

"It's hard to say just what she looked like," said Otho laughing, exposing the dark gap in the front of his mouth, "she looked like . . . a Dick Tiger with tits!"

As I entered the locker room, Otho, Rodell and I nodded mutely to each other—that's all I wanted, nothing more.

I kept to myself in the gym. I wasn't there to have a good time or make friends. I was there to fight. I didn't have anything clever to say, anyway. And I didn't want to waste my energy playing word games with these guys. I wanted to get myself in and out quickly.

Don't talk to me, I thought. Don't be polite. Don't try to make me feel nice. Don't relax. I'll wipe the smile off your face, pro or no pro. You think I don't know what's going on. You think I'm afraid to react. The joke's on you. Okay, I'll smile for you, but I'm biding my time, looking for the spot. You think no one can beat you. But I've been planning while you've been playing. I've been learning while you've been laughing. The game is almost over. It's time you acknowledged me. You're going to fall on the fucking floor not ever knowing what hit you.

I might have been overreacting but, for me, it was the only way. I had to approach each day in the gym as if it were a fight.

I didn't like to talk, so I just minded my own damn business. Words are windows into you. Besides, it's not good for a fighter to be a stutterer, as I was. They laugh at you and think you're scared.

The cacophony of Wilson Pickett suddenly ricocheted through the air. In walked Gypsy Joe Jackson cradling his chrome AM/FM/cassette/eight-track music box. He was wearing his usual wine-colored "gabs" and wine leather jacket.

"Gypsy, ma man!" shouted Otho.

"Peace, brother-cool!" squealed Gypsy, extending his hand for Otho to slap.

"What's hap'nen?" asked Gypsy.

Gypsy was a fighter with a face like a well-worn nickel, and his left eye, for some reason, was beginning to grow milky. Like Sugar Parker, Gypsy had once been a ranked welterweight, on the brink of a title shot, but a New York doctor discovered that he was totally blind in one eye. Till then, Gypsy had memorized eye charts. When he was banned from boxing, it was big news, and Gypsy's story and picture were the cover feature of *Sports Illustrated.*

But Gypsy still worked out occasionally. One of the strange

quirks about him was that on his athletic cup, he had painted a picture of a woman's panting face. He also had an odd habit of inserting a *Playboy* pinup inside his jock next to his cock. Those facts, however, were not revealed in *Sports Illustrated.* He was a weird guy.

Everyone except me looked like a fighter—Gypsy with his battered face, Otho with his toothless grin, Rodell with his lop-sided nostrils. The only scars I had were from a pediatrician. When I was seven years old, I had two nasty plantar warts removed from my left hand. One wart grew out of my middle knuckle, and the other wart jutted from the web. (I never chewed my warts, like other kids did, but my mother insisted that they looked "unsightly," so they were cut off.)

I looked at Gypsy's milky eye, and I felt like a mollycoddled white rich kid.

Fuck me, I thought.

While Otho bullshitted with Gypsy and Rodell about his up-coming fight in The Felt Forum with the hot, rising Puerto Rican star, Chu Chu Malave, I quietly unlocked the lock on my locker, an old army-green piece of metal that stood in the corner next to Brian O'Melia's locker. O'Melia, Chuck Wepner's chief spar-ring partner, was a pro heavyweight, big and beefy. I had spar-red O'Melia a few times and did pretty well. I broke his nose, in fact.

My lock combination was 4-18-26. It's funny the stupid things you remember.

Somebody should conduct a study on fighters' lockers. I'm not a psychologist, but I think that it's curious that the best fighters in Brandy's—Tyson, Gypsy, Jimmy Dupree and others—always kept, on the outside, the cleanest lockers. But their lockers *inside* were always a pig's mess. The inferior fighters—Rodell Dupree O'Melia, Bobby Kemmelman, Tom Sullivan and others, junked up the outside of their lockers with various trinkets and threaten-ing messages, but the insides were always as tidy as my Grandmother Bertha's closet. One fighter, Sullivan, an amateur with a 5–15 record, even sprayed the inside with English Leather cologne.

Once I observed this, I made certain my locker was clean outside and messy inside—like the good fighters.

My locker depressed me. Ever since I had read that "a self-confident person has a tendency to cross his T's higher when writing," I had begun crossing the "T" in "Peter" at the very top, or completely off the stem. It was the same motivation with my locker. As I stepped into my white wrestling shoes, I worried that everything about me had become a lie.

"Hey, man, go a coupla rounds?"

I looked up. It was Otho talking to me.

"S-sure," I stammered. I knew, however, that I was scheduled to spar three rounds with Hopkins. "It's okay with me, if it's okay with Tom," I managed to say without stuttering. I knew secretly that Tom would say no. Otho was too good for me. Let Tom be the bad guy, I told myself. Although I didn't want to have friends, I didn't care to make enemies.

I sat down on a wooden bench in the gym and waited for Hopkins to arrive. Taped on the wall above my head was a block-lettered sign:

THE MORE YOU SWEAT HERE
THE LESS YOU'LL BLEED IN THE RING

As I sat taping my hands, I listened to a pack of little old trolls sitting next to me. Some still had teeth, some didn't. All boxing gyms are soiled by these peculiar creatures.

Trolls are petulant old men who, in their youth, had always wished to be tough boxers but never possessed the necessary combative nature. In their latter years, having never solved this personality dilemma, they hang around boxing gyms compensating with tough-guy sneers and machismo attitudes. They usually have white hair and wear brown clothing. I've always felt that the main reason they congregated around gyms is that they hoped their feeble association with boxers would somehow enhance, or strengthen, their own lives. It's sad. They live each day believing their masculinity to be hollow.

They chew, or gum, toothpicks; they talk fights and sweat beer into their shirts each day from 3:00 P.M. to 8:00 P.M. in Brandy's Gym.

These boxing groupies were usually men who have been bus drivers, night watchmen and successful business executives. Sitting next to a pack of them is really a treat. Observing their John Wayne attitudes and listening to their verbal graffiti is an experience.

They defecate jokes: "Women make good pets." "Jews make good drum-skins."

As I sat eating the skin inside my cheek, I observed Sugar Parker grimace as he ta-ta-ta-ta-ed the peanut bag—a small black bag that resembled a testicle. He thrashed it.

I looked around the gym and watched other sweaty fighters, all deeply absorbed in their private little combats. The strange thought occurred to me that fighters are so necessarily crazy that not to be crazy would amount to another form of craziness.

In a boxing gym like Brandy's, a boxer with a touch of insanity was always considered a genius.

Sometimes Tom got, I don't know, poetic. He once said to me that a boxing gym, with its smelly vitality, is like a small factory where men's muscles are made. I liked that.

At first, the raw stench of Brandy's flew up my nostrils, but I quickly got used to it.

When I first trained in Brandy's my own sweat smelled bad, like rotten skunk cabbage. I was eating too much junk food— McDonald's hamburgers, pizza, French fries and donuts. But after a week of boxing, sweating and hitting the bags, my perspiration smelled almost sweet.

* * *

A cold trickle of sweat slid down the inside of my 15½ inch biceps. I perspire easily. I guess I was sweating partly because of the warmth radiating from all of the overheated bodies, and partly because I was nervous sparring Hopkins.

Fear squeezed my stomach, but you'd never have known it from looking at me.

I've been scared in a classroom, scared in a football game, scared at a family reunion, and, all in all, it is very much like being scared in a boxing gym. It is, in essence, being scared. And I hated it.

I yawned. I always felt tired before fighting, even sparring.

"Hey, Peter. What's up?"

Lazily, I looked over. It was Bobby Kemmelman.

"Hi!" I said, smiling. I was glad for the distraction. I hadn't seen Bobby in the gym since his loss. I glanced at his eyebrow and noticed that the long black zipper of stitches was still holding his eyebrow together. The scab that had formed looked like a long piece of bacon.

"Heard you won—good job!" he said, smiling. He punched my arm playfully. "You're in the quarter finals."

"Yeah," I said, apologetically.

"You're gonna go all the way, man!" he exclaimed.

"Bobby," I lied, "I was sure it was going to end up you against me."

"It's okay," he said, shrugging. "I never win anything anyways."

Embarrassed, I looked down. His fingernails, I noticed, were still filthy black.

"I thought I'd stop by and clue you in on the others," he said.

"Others?"

"The other middleweights—I did some scouting."

Two different people began fighting for control of my brain—one was a candy-ass white kid who used to have two warts on his left hand, slept with a teddy bear, wet the bed and sucked his thumb. He wanted to learn any scrap of data about the other fighters. The other person was a stoic fighter who had his blinders on.

"Don't matter," I said, yawning. I stood up and started shadowboxing.

"Let me tell you anyways," he said enthusiastically.

"First, ya got a white kid from Long Island—name's Capobianco—straight black hair—a left hooker. The way he fights, he must be converted, like you. Not to worry, you'll blow him away."

I knew whom he was referring to—the grinning fool who sat with that Neanderthal trainer—the clown who stared and smiled at me, trying to psyche me out before my first fight.

"Then you got Gillio—another white dude. He's one of the best. Real strong."

"Tattoo?" I asked, involuntarily.

"Yeah, on the arm—an eagle."

"The Navy guy," I said, throwing out a one-two.

"Navy *champ!*" corrected Bobby.

"Champ?" I blurted.

"That's what his brother said after his fight last week. Said he was twenty-five years old and All Navy Champ at Baton Rouge."

"The asshole isn't supposed to have fights," I said, grinning. My grin was the same lie I used in the ring when I got hit hard.

"But he's got no A.A.U. fights," explained Bobby. "I guess that's why they was able to sneak him into sub-novice."

"Bitch!" I said, punching my shadow on the wall.

"He's a fuckin' animal," added Bobby. "Guy's got a jaw like a rock. He knocked the guy out last week. I hope you don't draw him."

I wasn't too sure if Bobby, by telling me all this trash, was helping me much.

"Then there's Griffith . . . Emile's cousin."

"Emile's cousin?" I stopped dead in my tracks. "Emile's cousin?" I repeated. All I could envision was a kid living in a boxing gym learning all the professional tricks from Uncle Emile—a boxing great. The thought made me sick.

"He's good, real good," said Bobby softly. "He's only a fair boxer but he's a little more smart and a lot quicker and a bit stronger than most . . . and much meaner."

Screw this, I'm not listening any more, I thought.

"Then there's 'Sweetpea' Roundtree," continued Bobby. "He's the short black guy who wears those satin leopard trunks. Ever see him?"

I shook my head.

"Thinks he's Roberto Duran, this guy. Scowls and all. Punches good, but he's got short arms. I heard that he's Tom Bethea's sparring partner at Telstar Gym, but I can't swear to it."

Great, I thought—Tom "The Bomb" Bethea fought Nino Benvenuti for the middleweight championship. Besides, I hate fighting short guys. They were harder to get underneath and penetrate.

"Then ya got Centano," reported Bobby. "Truthfully, I don't know much about him 'cept he's tall and wears those shitty red tassles on his shoes, like Ali—looks cocky to me. His record's three wins with two k.o.'s."

I shadowboxed nervously as he spoke.

"Then there's a college kid—Pace University . . ."

"College kid?" I interrupted. "How you know all this?"

"Sandy Saddler, his trainer," said Bobby. "He told me. The fighter's name is Amen Jones—a real tall guy with a big fuckin' afro. If you cut his hair off, he'd still stand six-four."

"Huh." I grunted, as I boxed an eight-by-ten black-and-white glossy of Tony "Beer Barrel" Galento.

"You gotta watch this guy," warned Bobby.

"Who?" I asked.

"This college kid. It's like his punches have radar—everything he throws hits. He's one of the better ones."

Shit—I thought—they all sounded good.

"Lastly, you got the wimp—Americo Valero," Bobby said.

Valero was the same wimp who slashed Bobby's eyebrow.

"You wanna hear a laugh?" said Bobby. "I found out from Saddler—he's Valero's trainer, too—that Valero is a delivery boy in a grocery store!" Bobby chuckled to himself. "Imagine that. I got beat up by a New York City delivery boy!"

Bobby was smiling but I knew about those smiles.

"Bobby," I offered, "thanks for all that info. But, you know, I'll never forget one thing."

"What's that?"

"The time you almost ripped my brain out with that right-hand shot." I playfully grabbed him by his shoulders and shook.

A proud smile softly flickered across his face. I just wanted to make him feel better, that's all.

"Us Jews aren't good at fighting," sighed Bobby, "at least not with fists."

I didn't know Bobby was Jewish. I looked at him and smiled weakly. Secretly, I agreed. Jews read books, they didn't fight.

In Hebrew, I said, "God bless the Jews."

Bobby's eyes almost popped. He replied in Hebrew. "You're Jewish?"

"Not according to law," I said. I didn't know Bobby was a Hebe, but then again, he didn't know that I was either. At least half. My father was a Polish Jew.

Sometimes I felt as though I was boxing at half-strength, with only one side of myself—the Irish side. I boxed because I knew that someday I wanted to expose my softer artistic side—the Jew in me.

Bobby stripped off his blue working shirt, exposing his oily red-acned shoulder. I noticed he had gotten plumper.

"Too many blintzes, Bobby?" I asked.

He pinched the flab around his white belly and quipped, "Oy! 'Fat' is only a three-letter word invented to confuse people."

I laughed.

"I can eat as many blintzes, knishes or matzos as I want and not get fat," he said sighing, "as long as I don't swallow them."

I was about to ask Bobby if he knew anything about Tom's

little bottle. But that's when I saw Mudbone Hopkins gingerly skip into the gym.

When a fighter walks across a gym floor, he'd stand out like a sore thumb if he didn't appear callously unconcerned, or cold, or ready to punch somebody's lights out. But Hopkins—last year's N.Y. Golden Gloves Champion, and one of America's top amateur middleweights—was different.

He was definitely a dangerous dude. He could barge into any gym in the world, but instead, he gently eased by amateur fighters as they skipped rope.

He once told me, "People say I should do crazy things—be like Ali—but I ain't gonna do anything that ain't me. Mudbone Hopkins is Mudbone Hopkins."

Ten minutes crawled by before Mudbone finally emerged from the dressing room.

He wore his orange "Dance Disco" shirt, red woolen shorts and white leather boxing shoes with a red "H" stitched on each ankle.

Judging from Hopkins's lopsided nose and the thick white wormlike scars within his eyebrows, he was a fighter with a dream, and he was quite willing to pay the price for his dream.

But still, he was handsome in a craggy, masculine sort of way. There was masonry to his rugged face, scarred eyebrows, molded cheekbones and lantern jaw.

Hopkins sauntered up to me and gave me a "brother" handshake. Slowly, he unraveled his high-pitched voice, "How's ma man Mr. Watts today?" He smiled, showing two gold teeth.

"I'm okay, you?"

"Fine. I hear we's goin' three today."

"Well, I'll try," I laughed.

"Take it easy on me," laughed Hopkins. "Up today at five, been a long one." Hopkins worked as a city maintenance worker, cleaning and painting school buses.

He never asked me what I did for a living, though, and I didn't volunteer the information.

Fighters like Hopkins, who'd quit school and worked blue collar were resentful of guys like me, who were still in school. I never identified myself as a student. I was a janitor, or a mechanic, and we stayed friends. That's why when I drove to the gym, I hid my school textbooks beneath the front seat.

And that's why I sometimes used "ain't" or "sombitch" or slurred my words—to blend.

I was a fucking liar.

I don't know why, but suddenly there was a flash of lightning before my eyes, an internal rumble, and my mind caved in.

I stopped shadowboxing, and I asked myself, What the fuck am I doing here?

Suddenly, I wished that I was back in my stepfather's air-conditioned house. I visualized my mother and my stepfather and how much I hated and cursed them, but now, from this vantage point in Brandy's Gym, they didn't seem that bad. After all, they were just people doing their best.

GET OUT OF HERE! a voice inside me cried. Who was I kidding? I never really liked to box. That's why I secretly wished that I could kill somebody in the ring. That way, I could bow out gracefully.

I bit down on my mouthguard and tried to get a hold of myself. I shook my head and pretended that there was no such thing as an inner voice, or options, or fear—and if there were, I didn't have any of them.

With a private wince, I knew I wasn't *really* a fighter. I looked at the radical differences between myself and those tattooed boxers spitting, sweating and swearing alongside me.

Desire and loathing mixed within me.

WHAT POSSIBLE REASONS COULD I HAVE FOR BEING HERE? my brain screamed.

Maybe I'm boxing because I'm scared to argue and fight at home. Maybe it's because I'm scared to compete in school. Maybe it's because I'm a coward in real life.

I clamped my brain shut and refused to answer a damn thing.

It was like when my eyelids involuntarily closed before I was aware that a buzzing fly was about to enter my eye.

The bell clanged, Sugar Parker yelled and I gobbed a nice, thick clam onto the wooden floor. My thoughts went out with it. I twisted the soles of my Adidas wrestling shoes into my spit to get better traction.

I continued shadowboxing. Boxing shadows.

I watched Tom shuffle toward a desk. On top was a glass jar and in it were mouthpieces floating in a murky liquid like a medical exhibit. He fished one out, rinsed it in lukewarm water from a 7-Up bottle and stuffed it into Mudbone's mouth. Then Tom fit a greasy black leather "SPARTAN" headgear onto Mudbone's head. Mudbone swiveled his seventeen-inch neck to adjust it. His thick neck was an asset in absorbing punches.

Mudbone was scheduled to spar four men. First was Eddie Romero—an armed robber and eight-year man from Rikers Prison. Judging from his forearms, Romero loved nature: tigers, panthers and snakes.

Romero was a middleweight from San Juan. Before the bell he bounced nervously in his corner trying to hide the damp fear beneath his armpits.

The bell rang, and they touched gloves. Tom angrily shouted orders to Mudbone from the ring apron.

"Defense! Slip them punches! Side to side! Defense wit' this guy!"

For two rounds Mudbone did everything asked of him, plus gave Romero a bloody nose with a devastating double jab.

At the end of the second round, Tom whispered at the top of his lungs, with damaged vocal cords, "What's wrong wit' you? I tol' ya don't punch! Defense! Defense!" Mudbone shrugged. He knew part of Tom's job was to never appear satisfied.

Hopkins's second opponent didn't look like a sparring partner. In my humble opinion, it resembled an anthropomorphic specimen. Actually, its name was Larry "Tumbler" Davis, a 165-pound, five-foot, four-inch taxi driver and ex-pro.

Tumbler's torso appeared to have been poured from concrete. He stepped into his protective cup and between Vaseline-smeared lips, hollered, "I'm comin' outta retirement to face the next middleweight champion of the world." Hopkins sociably nodded his head.

The bell rang, and Tom instructed Mudbone to go on the offensive. Their sparring match was like two hurricanes in the same paper bag. A frightened opponent staring at their awesome physiques could understandably puke.

Everyone in the gym stopped and watched this one, even Lola, the bald, grunting lady.

Blood and water sprayed down on the old trolls sitting at ringside as the two middleweights landed punches. I could hear the leather pop and could almost feel the punches, and in a minute, I would.

The Tumbler had a right hand like a Mack truck, and he fought as scientifically as a sledgehammer. After two furious rounds, the Tumbler tumbled out of the ring with bloody teeth.

"Man!" he mumbled, "the inside o' my nose feel like peanut brittle!"

Benny, Tom's brother and co-trainer, wiped Tumbler's face clean and handed him a ten-dollar bill.

"Good workout. See you tomorrow."

Hopkins was just warming up. His third sparring partner, Speedy Clover, was a pro light-heavy who had fought all over Europe.

Although this match was not as animal as the previous one, it highlighted Hopkins's prime assets: punching power, deftly executed combinations and speed.

I loved watching Hopkins, he was beautiful. He did things with his hands that were incredible. But Clover was quick, too— quick, cute and cocky. At times, he spun Hopkins and made him look silly. After two rounds of Clover's freshness, Hopkins landed a left hook which sunk into Clover's jaw. One more punch and Clover's mouthguard sprawled out.

"Time!" yelled Tom, climbing the ring steps. "Hopkins! You're boxin' worse each day, and right now, you're boxin' like next month."

Benny picked up Clover's mouthpiece and, stepping on the lower strand of the ring rope, carefully guided Clover out the ring.

"I'm okay, I'm okay," Clover insisted as he tripped down the steps.

"Climb in there, Pete, you're next," said Tom, checking the Vaseline around Hopkins's eyes.

With abdominals fluttering, I stood my manic self up and climbed into the ring. I adjusted my headgear, a real thin thing that didn't absorb much, but that's the way I wanted it.

"Three rounds," said Tom.

I nodded my head.

The bell rang.

I know it might sound strange coming from me, but it's always a war when I fight. Even in the gym, when I spar, I *need* to go all out. I learned early with a fighter named Carter Williams, that if I am not aggressive, I get busted up. I'm not Joe Frazier, but I've read that it's the same with him, too.

The trolls always enjoy watching me fight. They really liked it the day I broke O'Melia's nose with a right uppercut. Man, so did I.

But I didn't enjoy climbing in with Hopkins. He was a little too dangerous. Although we were both middleweights, his height and reach were both three inches more than mine.

Even though I fought him hard, I never hurt him. He had the skill to toy with me. I'd try my best to take him out, but he'd always draw back, and my punches would fall short by inches.

At the end of the first round, he tapped me on the top of the head playfully. It was like I was a little boy or something, and it always pissed me off.

It *is* the longest three minutes in the world, especially when you have asthma and all you're doing is thwomping and thwacking air.

But during the second round that's not all I was doing. Despite getting a spanking, I was learning and gaining confidence. I saw moves and strategies most people didn't even know existed—six punch combinations, left uppercuts, elbow blocks, feet feints and a pile-driving left jab delivered from the waist.

The bell rang for the third, and we touched gloves. This was only my third round and already I was tired, more than him, it appeared.

I dogged forward, bobbing and weaving, concentrating—anticipating his right hand. I wanted to throw a counter left. He skipped and bounced quickly. Suddenly he loosened his jab, flinging it from his svelte thirty-inch waist—POP-POP-POP! Then, without warning, his next jab turned into a hook, and he fired two powerful lefts, another right cross and a left uppercut. He danced back, shot out the right again and automatically, cutely, stepped to the side, avoiding my awkward rush. Moves like these probably made the old trolls at ringside come in their pants. They probably thought these classic moves had been lost to antiquity. But they weren't; Hopkins was using them on my head.

I felt embarrassed for getting hit so much. My face felt red-hot like it had just been boiled. It probably looked like that, too.

But if I could claim one small thing, it was this—he never hurt me. That's because he wasn't trying or because he was tired from the first three sparring partners—that's a gracious thought, I told myself. I always praised myself when I had one of those.

Toward the end of the round, Hopkins stood flat-footed and started spraying punches. It was like a runner sprinting the last fifty yards. I crouched inside, held my gloves close to my face and kept an eye on his best punch—the right. When he let up, I squirted in a quick left hook. It bounced into his jaw, and it seemed to take the bones from his legs. He grabbed me by the biceps and clinched.

"What you tryin' to do, knock me out?" he mumbled.

Just then, the bell rang.

"Good round!" shouted Tom. "My two middleweight champs right here!"

"Good round," mumbled Hopkins.

"You, too," I gasped.

At the end of that round, he didn't tap me on top of the head. I tapped him.

Tom unlaced the fat sixteen-ounce gloves and helped me stuff my taped fists into smaller bag-gloves.

"Get on a heavy bag," he instructed.

I looked around, but all were taken. Otho was on one, Rodell on another, and a light-heavy named Sullivan was pummeling the third.

"Being used," I said.

Tom shuffled up to Sullivan and tapped him on the shoulder. "Give this to Pete," he ordered.

Sullivan looked at Tom with a juvenile delinquent expression.

"Get off! I want Watt on it," Tom repeated.

I knew how Sullivan felt; I had felt that way in algebra class many times.

Sullivan looked at me and said, "Anyone ever tell you that when you fight, you look like Joe Frazier?"

"No," I said, flattered.

"Well, that's because you don't," he said.

I tried to think of a quick comeback. When I couldn't, I feinted a right hand to his face.

"A joke! A joke!" he whined, flinching.

That's how a lot of my two hundred street fights started, a guy gets smart.

The bell rang. I snapped out a quick jab. I always tried to be the first one in the gym to begin working.

I loved the heavy bag, it didn't move or punch back.

Fortissimo thumps resounded as my knuckle walloped and smacked the one-hundred-pound bag. My fists zipped with combinations—the bag grunted on its chain.

Tom barked instructions—I could hardly hear him above the noise.

"Give yourself room. Make him jab to your right, then slip to your right—left hook to the body."

Like an apt pupil, I did what I was told. Wet dribbles scribbled down my forehead. Giving myself room, I jabbed. Jabjab-step-jabjabjab. Then, chin tucked beside my shoulder, I stepped in and exploded a lean left hook into the bag's belly.

"GOOD!" said Tom.

Out the corner of my eye, I noticed a few trolls strolling over to take a closer look at me.

"Punch hard—HARD! Punch *through* it, not at it"! Tom said.

Working the bag was serious business. I never allowed myself to relax or to swing it around for a better angle. I never leaned my head against it or let my elbows touch. All that was cute, but pure shit. I moved constantly and never threw less than three punches at one time. THE MORE YOU SWEAT HERE—THE LESS YOU BLEED IN THE RING.

My imaginary opponent was always in front of me, and my hands were always held high. I punched hard and long. My stomach felt like it was going to fall out, but I didn't obey the pain, I kept going. Lefts-rights-lefts-rights . . .

Let's face it, I knew I wasn't going to win the title on technique or talent. I had to make up for it with punching power, aggressiveness and brute force.

CLANG!

"Good! shouted Tom, smiling. "Yeah! My pet tiger!"

Wet with sweat and puffing for oxygen, I circled the bag.

I enjoyed the trolls staring at me. After the thousands of rounds alone in my basement and in the gym, I was grateful for attention.

"Am I too easy on him?" Tom asked his brother Benny.

"Yeah, make him work harder," answered a troll.

"Okay, you heard him," said Tom. "If you wanna be champ, you gotta work harder."

I breathed deeply, damn asthma. I had one short minute to rest. I reminded myself to ask Tom later what that stuff was in his bottle.

CLANG!

"Work!" barked Tom. "Practice that straight right."

Because I was converted, the right was the toughest to master. "Pivot that foot!"

I plopped right hands repeatedly into my imaginary opponent's body and chin.

"Boxin' is mostly mental," I overheard Tom explain to a troll. "It ain't as physical as people think. And it's easier when you don't got to work on confidence . . . PUNCH *THROUGH* THE BAG! . . . like I said, you gotta believe in yourself. No matter how much skill you got, you can't execute unless you have the mental toughness. That's Pete's biggest asset—his belief in himself."

Little did he know, I secretly thought.

When the bell finally rang, I stood in a puddle of sweat, panting. I still hadn't gotten the straight right correct.

"Here, look . . . ," said Tom, assuming his archaic 1930 boxing stance. He tapped his shoulder. "From the shoulder, look . . ." He snapped off a straight right, just like, probably, Tony Canzoneri. "Your body's like a garden gate, see? Turn it! Pivot and catch your weight on your left foot." Tom looked at the trolls. "He's converted, it don't come natural."

I tried it a few times. So did the trolls.

"Okay, how many you go so far?" asked Tom.

"Three sparring, three on the bag," I puffed.

"Do one more here—work on the thirteen basic moves I taught ya. Then we'll do three on the light bag."

The thirteen basic moves were Tom's creation. I practiced them endlessly and could perform then in my sleep.

CLANG!

One . . . double jab (you could mix it up, body-head, head-body, etc.) . . . Two . . . left hook to body—right to head . . . Three . . . right hook to body—left hook to head . . . Four . . . left hook to body—left hook to face . . . Five . . . right (uppercut or hook) to body—right to face . . . Six . . . jab to face—right to body—left hook to body . . . Seven . . . daydreaming, a thought like a splinter entered my mind. I remembered the time I saw a woman try to kill her own son. That's what it looked like when I peeked into the window. The boy was strung up by his wrists and ankles with the rubber cord from the vacuum cleaner. She had him tied to the bottom of the staircase and was whipping him red with a coat hanger. I knew the lady. I didn't think of her in these terms. She was my mother. And the bloody little boy sobbing and twitching in a heap was my older brother, Daniel. I shoved the thought roughly aside . . . Eight . . . jab to the face—right to the head—left hook to the head . . . Nine . . . place your forehead on bag and dig six strong uppercuts to body—finish with a quick flurry of six uppercuts—jab . . . Ten . . . parry imaginary jab-counter with own jab . . . Eleven . . . parry imaginary jab—counter with right hand to head . . . Twelve . . . parry imaginary right hand—counter with jab . . . Thirteen . . . parry imaginary right hand—counter with own right hand.

CLANG!

I stood limply as Tom wiped my face dry with a gray Holiday Inn towel.

"You look good, but you ain't in top shape yet, only fifty percent," said Tom. "How's your lungs?"

"Okay," I said tiredly.

"Your *muchacho* gets tired quickly," said a loud voice from the crowd. "How'd he do against a mover?" It was a troll with a badly broken nose. He looked like a former fighter; either that, or he had it smashed in a car accident.

"What's that?" asked Tom. Someone had forgotten to tell him that trolls weren't supposed to interfere with workouts.

I looked at the broken-faced troll. He hunched himself inside a gray tattered coat, and a splotch of something or other soiled his lapel.

"How would he do against a guy who dances?" asked the gnome.

"Knock him out, what else?" shot Tom indignantly.

"Even a *muchacho* who uses the whole ring?"

I never noticed this guy before. Most of them in Brandy's were Caucasian, not Latinos, like him.

"You seen this guy fight," said Tom. "He'd be in his fuckin' chest!"

"I mean someone who moves from side to side and shoots punches like Ali."

Tom waved his hand, laughed, and said, "Ali farts dust."

I grinned and remembered the graffiti on the bathroom wall. Had Tom written it, I wondered?

Tom jutted his whiskered chin towards the light bag. Breathing deeply, I walked toward it. It hung in the corner next to the wall with the full-length mirrors.

Boxers are the most egotistical bastards in the world. If one fighter is hitting a bag or shadowboxing in a mirror, and another fighter walks by and their eyes happen to meet, each is sure that the other guy's been watching and sizing him up. I know because I'm the same way.

"I want three good rounds," ordered Tom.

Poised next to the bag, waiting for the bell, I stuck out my mouthpiece and manipulated it with my teeth. It was something to do. Unlike other fighters, I wore my mouthguard during the bags. I wanted to simulate fight conditions as much as possible.

CLANG!

"Work!" said Tom. But I already was on my third punch.

My fists rolled in smooth circles—TA-TA-TA-TA, then T-T-T-T-T.

It's easy to cheat on this bag. If you get tired, you have a tendency to take potshots at it—uppercuts, straight rights and left hooks. If you time them right, they look sharp, but people in the know know you're cheating.

"C'MON! Agitate that bag of wind!" yelled Tom.

If you hit the light bag right, you don't even need to look at it. Sometimes I glanced at the torn centerfold picture of growling George Foreman or a hand-lettered sign that read:

WHEN THE GOING GETS TOUGH,
THE TOUGH GET GOING!!!
—Tom Brandy

By the beginning of the third round, I was again standing (or treading in place) in a sweat puddle.

My hot breath could have melted a candy bar. I thrashed the damn bag into a machine-gun noise. Threads of sweat sprayed from my hair, off my arms and into the bag's blurred arc.

As the bell clanged, I launched a brutal right hand to finish off my imaginary opponent. It missed.

"Shit!" I panted.

"No problem, tiger!" said Tom. "Good round."

Disgusted, I held one nostril closed and blew a hurricane of snot onto the floor. It was a good round, yeah, but I didn't have to mess it up by missing at the end. I always fuck up things at the end. Was I another Max Streets, I wondered.

"Ever hear of a fighter named Max Streets?" I asked Tom.

Tom gave me a look, then wiped my face dry and draped the damp towel over his shoulder.

"Finish up with your exercises," said Tom. I watched as he fished for something in his hip pocket. For a second, I thought it was that bottle. But instead, he brought out a roll of Lifesavers. He thumbed one up.

"Open!" he ordered.

I opened my mouth, and he popped in a green one.

"For reward," he said.

Some of the trolls laughed.

"Like givin' a horse sugar!" remarked one.

"Like givin' a dog a bone!" snapped Tom. Shuffling away, he muttered, "He never refuses it."

My first exercise was a neck isometric. I used to do a football exercise, but this one that I had devised was better. I folded a towel, placed it on the end of a bench and positioned my head so that only the top of my forehead touched. Then I placed my body in a push-up position. With only forehead and toes touching, I held this position for a three-hundred count. I did the same two more times, working each side of my neck. It was a tough exercise, but clearing out the lazy trolls from the bench was the hardest part.

For my stomach, I sat on the ring apron. I held my body at a forty-five-degree angle sit-up position. Hands behind my head, elbows back, I held this for a slow six-hundred count.

At the count of four hundred, Hopkins sauntered up to me, lifted my sleeveless t-shirt and pinched me in the gut.

"Ow!"

"Who's your favorite team, man?" he asked smiling.

"Why?" I asked.

"Just tell me—who's your favorite team?"

"White Sox," I grunted, trying not to lose count.

"White Sox? That ain't right," he muttered.

"It ain't?" I asked.

"No!" he said, putting his hand on my shoulder. "**You're** your favorite **team!**"

"Oh, yeah," I said, losing my count.

"C'mon, say it."

I figured I was about at five hundred, so for punishment for losing the count, I started at four hundred and fifty.

"C'mon, say it," said Hopkins.

"Me," I said.

"All of it—me, I'm my favorite team," he goaded.

"Me—I'm my favorite team," I said.

"You got it now, ma man!" sung Hopkins. Then the bastard, grinning, tapped me on top of the head.

In strolled a behemoth white guy wearing a black fedora. Banging the wooden door, he yelled, "I'm Chuck Fucking Wepner, and I'm the baddest motherfucker in this here gym!"

It was Chuck Wepner.

If the mark of a good fighter is not having marks, then Chuck Wepner was definitely in the wrong profession.

When Chuck dies, his exquisitely scarred-up face should be preserved in a bottle of formaldehyde.

His flat, fleshy raisin-nose was squished into both cheeks, and the soft, marshmallow flesh around his eyebrows was as thin as balloonskin. He had had so many cuts and stitches in his eyebrows that the hair there had refused to grow back.

In my humble opinion, his remaining face was a demilitarized zone.

After the Liston fight, in which Chuck received thirty-two stitches, Tom took extra special precautions when wiping off Chuck's face during workouts. Tom dabbed gingerly at the eyes, always using the soft, fluffy side of the towel.

I was almost finished with my workout—I hopped off the ring apron and shot off thirty quick push-ups. Then I walked up to Chuck. I wanted to find out if he knew anything about Tom's little bottle. He was in the middle of an interview with a *Jersey City Journal* reporter, so I sat down and listened.

"Who was the toughest opponent I faced?" asked Chuck.

The reporter nodded.

Chuck scratched his chest hair, a curly thicket that peeked out from his half-buttoned red silken shirt, and thought.

"Stallings. Stallings was tough," he answered finally. "But the hardest I got hit was against Foreman. George hurt me. My head went like this." Chuck did a 360-degree spin with his finger. "But it's funny, Sonny Liston punches much harder than Foreman. Liston punches so hard he should be outlawed. But when he hit me, the pain, ya know, didn't register." Chuck shrugged and laughed.

"Chuck," said the reporter delicately, "you've been around a long time, let's see . . . since 1963 . . ."

"Sixty-four," corrected Chuck, tugging at his Fu Manchu mustache.

"Nineteen sixty-four, that's correct. What's your chance of getting a crack at the world title?

"I've been around a long time, but I know I'm gettin' better each year. So my chances are good. I'm still learning."

"How old are you?" asked the reporter.

"Thirty."

"You look older, Chuck," said the reporter tentatively.

"People say that—they say I look forty. It's the scars. But I've been soaking my face in brine, so you know . . ."

"Chuck, how much more time do you have before you call it quits?" asked the reporter.

Chuck responded by laughing good-naturedly. "They all want to know how many miles I got left. It's like I'm a truck or somethin'."

"Four-wheel drive!" exclaimed an exuberant troll.

"I'll tell you what," said Chuck suddenly serious. "You tell your readers that Chuck Fucking Wepner is so tough that even when he gets knocked down, he hits the canvas. You tell them that."

Chuck picked up his gym bag and headed towards the dressing room.

"Chuck," I called.

"Pete! How's it hangin'?" he said. "You workout?"

"Yeah—went three with Mudbone," I said—as if he was really interested, I thought.

"I hear you and Hopkins are shoo-ins for the Gloves."

I shrugged.

"I was a Golden Glove champ myself," said Chuck.

"You knocked out Johnny Clohessy in the first," I said.

"That's right!" beamed Wepner. "You remember!"

"Chuck, I want to ask you something."

"Shoot."

"You know anything about Tom's bottle?"

"Bottle?" asked Chuck.

I watched his face for a reaction. Like most fighters, Chuck was a noisy nose breather—but he took the cake. I listened to him breathe—that was the only reaction I got.

"A bottle from his hip pocket," I added.

He shook his head slowly. "I don't know anything about that bottle." Breathing noisily through deviated septums, he stepped into the dressing room, hunched his shoulders and said, "Sorry."

* * *

"Tom, what's in the bottle?" I asked.

Tom looked over his shoulder as he tugged an uncooperative bag-glove off Prince Lola's sweaty hand.

"Can't ya see I'm busy?" he said.

"Yeah, loverboy, can't ya see he's busy?" parroted Lola. I recoiled a bit at the weird, scuzzy world I saw swimming in her pretty brown eyes. I gave them time to finish their task, then repeated, "Tom, what's in the bottle?"

He winked.

"Tom, really, I want to know—what's in the bottle?"

"What's in the bottle, what's in the bottle, everyone wants to know what's in the bottle," he said walking away impatiently. "Sorry, I don't give out secrets."

I grabbed his t-shirt. "Tell me, is it legal?"

"Is what legal?"

"What's in it?"

"What are you worried about?"

"I want to know what I'm drinking, that's all."

Tapping his hip pocket, Tom said, "People have been trying to find out my ingredients for decades, and now I'm supposed to tell you? What's your problem? I wouldn't do anything to hurt you—you're my fighter."

Somewhat relieved, I smiled. It wasn't an answer, but for now it had to do.

"If I was you, I'd worry about throwing my right hand better," said Tom.

"I'm getting the hang of it," I said throwing it out for his inspection.

"Ain't bad," said Tom. "You think you're getting the feel of it?"

"Yeah," I said, snapping it out.

Whereupon Prince Lola grabbed her crotch and blurted, "Well, feel this then!"

"I know what's in that bottle," muttered Jack Sullivan, the light-heavyweight, unlacing his boxing shoes in the dressing room.

"What?" I asked.

"What's it worth to you?" Sullivan was always the wise-ass. I tried, but couldn't think of a smart retort.

"You got eardrums? What's it worth to you?" he repeated.

"You tell me, and I won't beat you up anymore," I joked—that was the best I could come up with.

"You never beat me up in your life," spat Sullivan, still unlacing his high-top shoes.

"Where'd you get that black eye then?" I asked.

"In a candy store," he said. "Look—if I told you what was in it you wouldn't believe me."

"Try me."

Sullivan sat up in his metal chair, looked to see if the coast was clear and whispered, "Each night, after all the fighters go home and no one is around, Tom collects all the towels that only the good fighters used—only the good fighters—then he squeezes them into tight knots to get out all the sweat. Then he drops all the sweat into the bottle and . . ."

"Screw you," I said.

"It's true! He's got sweat from Canzoneri and Barahona and Liston and Marciano and . . ."

"Up yours, Sullivan," I said.

"It's true, I tell you. But that's not all. Testosterone is in that there bottle. Ever hear of it?"

"Yeah, I've heard of it," I lied.

"Testosterone—the stuff that gives ya muscles and whiskers and a deep voice."

"Yeah, yeah," I said.

"Well, in that bottle is liquid testosterone," said Sullivan, slipping off his green trunks. He pulled down his jockstrap and grabbed his cock. "What Tom does is jack off into the bottle . . ."

"You asshole." This was the exact reason why I didn't talk to people in the gym.

"Sweat and cum. That's what you're drinkin', pal," said Sullivan, laughing.

I stalked toward him.

"Hey, it was a joke! Can't you take a joke?" he whined.

I patted him softly on the cheek and made a mental note to thoroughly pulverize him the next time we sparred. That damn bottle really bothered me. I didn't want to wake up in the morning and find out I was dead.

Resting with a white towel draped over my head (so I didn't have to look at anybody), I felt a bit woozy. I slumped comfortably in a metal chair and waited quietly for Rodell to finish showering.

I felt wilted because one-half of me was still lying on the gym floor in wet puddles.

Tom jutted his battered head inside the dressing room doorway and eyed the fighters.

"Hey, Parker!" he called. "When're you gonna get your ass in gear, huh?"

"What you mean?" asked Parker, who was sprawled comfortably on the floor.

"You know what I mean," said Tom. "You were dogging it today."

"I's tired, man," cried Sugar.

"Tired? Tough shit!"

"Oh, that's cold!" Sugar said.

"When the going gets tough, the tough get going!" Tom barked.

"When the going gets tough," said Sugar, "I do drugs."

I peeked from beneath my towel at Sugar's arms. He wasn't kidding. I've seen those marks before—on my brother Dan's arm.

Everyone knew Sugar was a junkie but Tom.

"Okay, you lazy bum," said Tom. "You can joke, but clean up your act or no more fights." Tom eyed the other fighters and attempted to lighten things up by saying, "And remember, guys, no more tinkling in the showers—I know you do it."

When Tom left, Rodell pulled open the filthy shower curtain, grinned and said, "You mean piss?" And his cock suddenly jumped up and sprouted a leak, wet and yellow.

The shower stall in Brandy's gave everyone pause. We all feared it—even the toughest and most confident fighters. Everyone was secretly concerned about the germs, scabies and ringworms that lurked in there. We all tiptoed in and tiptoed out, hoping for the best. I guess the smart thing to do would have been to wear rubber thongs, but that would have been admitting weakness.

The thing that unnerved me most about the stall was the thick, cheeselike sludge on the floor. I hated that. I think that sludge was what was responsible for the wicked, raw sewerage smell. I didn't mind the flowery shower curtain encrusted with black mildew or the slimy tiled walls or the temperamental hot water —or cockroaches—it was the filthy, glutinous sludge that got to me. And people pissing in there. I didn't like that much, either—even though I did it myself.

It smelled like rancid garbage, but what the fuck, I had to shower. Tiptoeing in gingerly and arching my back to avoid the slick shower curtain, I adjusted the temperature so that the water was much hotter than I really wanted. I did this partly for punishment (for missing the right hand on the speed bag) and partly because I didn't want to indulge myself. Minor punishment, self-induced, always made me feel one-up on my competition.

After showering, I tiptoed out of the stall and dressed quickly. I made certain that my hair was good and dry before walking outside.

Before leaving, I said goodbye to Tom and Mudbone. I looked around, but didn't see Kemmelman.

"See you tomorrow," I said, shaking Mudbone's meaty hand with the five talented knuckles.

"Sounds good," he said, smiling. "Hey! Who's your favorite team?"

"Me—I'm my favorite team," I said.

As I trotted down the rickety wooden steps toward my black Pontiac that had *The Norton Anthology of Poetry* and *Mastering Spanish* tucked beneath the front seat, I thought, I'm going to be all right. I'm going to be all right—as long as I don't listen to that human being inside of me.

Driving home, I stopped my car at the red light on John F. Kennedy Boulevard and concentrated on squeezing the rubber spaldeen that strengthened my forearms. I could see myself . . . the Golden Gloves champion! . . . gloves raised in triumph . . . THE CHAMP! . . . the wonderful Madison Square Garden crowd—the best in the world—giving me a standing-O! . . . Valerie loving me from ringside . . . my proud father cheering . . . my entire high school going ape-shit . . . signing autographs . . .

The light turned green and I slapped myself back into my habitual inferiority. Fuck me and my fucking ego.

I've got all of Muhammed Ali's ego but none of his genius; all of Floyd Patterson's insecurities but none of his talent; all of Willy Pastrano's hand wringing but none of his grace; all of Battling Siki's craziness but none of his courage.

That night, after eating dinner, after my three miles of roadwork and after "All In the Family" and "Twilight Zone," I went to bed and couldn't sleep.

It occurred to me at about 2:00 A.M., that I didn't know who the fuck I was.

I wasn't really a fighter, and I wasn't really a student. I wasn't really Jewish, and I wasn't really Christian. Fighting converted, I wasn't really lefty, and I wasn't really righty. I didn't really belong with this family, and I didn't really belong with my father's new family.

I knew one thing before I fell off at 3:00 A.M.—I was *really* a fucked-up adolescent. *Really.*

EIGHT

VALERIE

Chocolate Donuts

I watched Valerie trot toward the house. Her long black hair tossed in the cold wind. Like black satin, it tousled about her shoulders and flipped down her back. I gazed at her thin thighs and pink knees below her cotton miniskirt. I wondered why pretty girls, like Valerie, dated football stars, or boxers, like myself. If she only knew how weak I truly was, I thought.

An icy gust swept past as I opened the front door.

"H-H-hello!" she shivered. White ghosts swirled from her mouth as she breathed.

"Hi, there," I said.

"I'm BBBRRR!" she said, coquettishly nestling her chin into her rabbit fur coat.

"Come on in," I said.

"I don't know if I should. You might try to take advantage of a sweet young thing like me. But I got out of study hall so that you could, if you wanted to." She winked and stepped inside.

As I helped her slip off her jacket, I noticed the flirtatious way in which she arched her back and jutted out her proud little breasts. She then tiptoed in front of me and wrapped her arms around my neck.

"How's my big, tough boxer?" she cooed, pressing her petite body firmly into mine.

I looked at the circumference of her delicate face, her soft lips and cashmere eyes. She was a definite knockout. And one of the most improbably oversexed girls I had ever met.

"Well, are you?" she asked. Her voice was gentle and sexy, like a caress.

"Am I what?" I asked.

"Going to take advantage of me?"

I felt her uplifted breasts squish against my flannel shirt. The tickling sensation in my abdomen wasn't wholly unpleasant. I smelled her sweet perfume. She was wearing her black lacy panties. I was sure of it.

"I can't," I said, swiveling my neck like a fighter. I unsuccessfully ignored the stiffening in my pants.

"Please?" she pouted.

Even though I very much wanted to feel under her miniskirt, I stepped back and removed her arms from my neck.

Valerie Clinton was uncommonly beautiful. I loved her. I *think* I loved her. She was a mirror into which I looked and saw myself five times bigger than I really was. She was the clean-cut, gum-chewing, slim-hipped girl whom everyone in school secretly masturbated to—even teachers. She was a bouncy sixteen-year-old cheerleader and a straight-B student. But she wasn't the innocent little waif everyone assumed. Her nights weren't always devoted to homework.

I never told this to anyone, but one summer evening, Valerie persuaded me to drive to Tallman State Park. When we arrived, she hopped out of my Pontiac, and in the middle of the dimly lit road, in front of the headlights, I watched her peel off her blue jeans and black lacy underpants. She had wanted to do it right there in the middle of the road. So we did

Valerie loved sex. And occasionally she loved sex while dropping acid. That part I didn't like—the sex was fine.

"Let's fuck," she whispered.

I studied her large brown eyes to see if she was high. She wasn't. She was just normal.

"L-let me remind you how it is," I said. "I'm a fighter. Tonight I have a fight. I can't screw around." (I was pretending that I was on a TV screen and my future opponents were watching me spurning temptation.)

"How can you resist a hot little girl like me?" she asked.

"It's tough," I admitted.

"Oh well, your loss," she sniffed, squeaking her way into the kitchen with her rubber-soled tennis shoes. "What's to eat . . . anything?"

I offered her some chocolate donuts and a glass of milk.

Valerie eyed me over her donut and said, "I came here for a piece of your beautiful body and all you give me is milk and a donut?"

I gazed at her and realized that sex was undoubtedly her prime motivational force. I wondered what other aspirations or dreams she had. Did Valerie ever look beyond the next party?

"If that's what you're here for," I said, "maybe you should leave."

Suddenly, her snide expression dropped, and she looked at me seriously. "Well, actually, I came for one other reason."

"Oh?"

"I don't know if I should show this to you," she said, reaching into her leather purse. "I know you're a grouch before fights."

"What is it?"

"Did you see the interview?" she asked.

I remembered the *Daily News* reporter interviewing Tom and me. "I was wondering when that was coming out."

She handed me a newspaper. "Well, there's an interview, all right, on page fifty-six, but it's not about you."

VALERO WANTS FRESH PREY
By Dick Mackle

New York—Subnovice hopeful Americo Valero says the remaining fighters in his 160-pound division can only "dream" about winning the title on March 21st in Madison Square Garden.

Valero, undefeated in three fights, said he'll turn tonight's bout into a "nightmare" for his opponent. "I want to stand in the middle of the ring," said Valero. "He'll hit me, then I'll hit him, then he'll hit me, then I'll hit him, then I'll hit him, then I'll hit him, then I'll hit him. That will work out fine," said Valero, a twenty-six-year-old Dominican who decisioned his last opponent, Sweet-Pea Roundtree of Staten Island.

A grocery clerk, Valero says he isn't worried about meeting his sparring partner, Amen Jones, also of N.Y. Recreation. "Amen don't scare me none. We spar in the gym. I want fresh prey." Valero added, "I don't like to sound like I'm boasting, but I don't think there's anything out there for me. I anticipated that my toughest fight would be Pete Watt, but after seeing him, I think I was wrong. He's too pretty to be a fighter. I plan on altering his face and busting up his intestines."

Watt, who claims to be from Jersey City, kayoed Jamal Green, another N.Y. Rec fighter and Valero's sparring partner, in the second round.

"I'm smart," says Valero. "I have mental power over guys. My physical power has nothing to do with it, it just puts me into the ring. My mental power is what takes over everything."

The quarterfinals begin tonight at 8:00 at the Felt Forum.

I looked up at Valerie. "He sounds upset."

"He sounds underbred, if you ask me," she said.

I flipped the newspaper aside and looked at the pads of my fingertips. They were damp and dark with ink.

"He wants to bust up your intestines," she murmured.

"I can read," I snapped, wiping my hands on my blue jeans.

"I hope you're not mad at me for showing it to you."

"No," I said, "he's just a . . . tongue."

"And it's too big for his brain, if you ask me." Then Valerie looked at me earnestly and said, "Pete . . . I don't know why you got yourself involved with this awful tournament. All those dumb boxers trying to punch you, I'm frightened for you, you might get hurt. Sometimes I think that . . ."

"I should quit?"

"I didn't say that."

"It's what you were thinking," I said, realizing that it was certainly my own thought. Suddenly, I felt exposed. I looked at my miserable, naked inner self with repugnance and quickly erased the image, knowing that it was sure to reappear in another five minutes.

Again, I wondered what Valerie ever saw in me. Maybe I was her security, her trophy, her status, I don't know. But I was not the big moose she thought I was. Part of me wanted to tell her the truth, and part of me wanted to keep lying.

"Let's talk about something else, okay, Valerie?" I said.

"Well," she said, "thanks for the donut."

I watched as she silently dabbed the crumbs with her finger. All week I had wanted one of those chocolate donuts. But I knew in my heart that if I had eaten one, I'd have shoveled in five, and I had to make weight.

"Aren't you going to eat something?" asked Valerie, nibbling at a crumb.

"I'm waiting till three o'clock."

"And what does a he-man fighter, such as yourself, eat—root vegetables, bones and raw meat?"

"Mutton and porridge," I joked.

"No gruel?"

To answer properly, I handed Valerie my day's schedule which I had written on the flipside of a Rutgers University application form. In a fit of stupidity, I had sent away for the university catalogue and had intended to fill out the application, but I guess I had gotten involved with the boxing, and besides, my grades stunk and I didn't know what to study in college and I couldn't even make sense of the crazy catalogue . . .

⌐lots¬

10:30 — breakfast—eat 1 egg, 1 piece bread, honey, OJ, tea, sugar
11:00 — rest—put clothes in washing machine—(remember John Booth & my father)
12:00 — put clothes in dryer—cut hair—clip nails—weigh myself
12:30 — take clothes out of dryer
1:00 — TV—relax—"Jeopardy," "Candid Camera," "Password," "Andy Griffith Show"
3:00 — lunch—steak (rare) chew good—1 piece stale bread, spinach—tea (honey & sugar)—OJ
4:00 — Pray at Protestant Church
4:30 — walk to town—buy apple & Hershey candy bar (no almonds) take 15 min walk (eat apple)—drive home—study strategy before going to gym—make sure I have—

1) correct socks	5) mouthguard
2) shoes	6) white towel
3) jock & cup	7) hand bandages
4) trunks	8) robe

(wear undershirt under an undershirt)
5:30 — drive to gym—bring candy bar (eat it at 7:00)
6:00 — be at gym—weigh myself

"Why did you write everything down?" asked Valerie.
"I put myself on automatic."
"Automatic?" She looked at me closely. "I'm worried about you. You're brooding and all by yourself the whole day and all you think about is fighting. You're missing life—all the fun. You're getting too intense. I haven't seen you laugh in two

months. When was the last dance you went to? The last movie? The last rally? This is your senior year and you haven't been to a party yet! How can you do it?"

"I d-do it because I want to do it," I said, not really certain if that was the truth or not. She was the carefree, happy-go-lucky type. She wouldn't understand, I thought.

"Well, it's embarrassing to go to a party alone," she said.

"What's wrong with being alone?" I asked.

"Nothing," she said, defensively.

"Well, you have to go alone for a while."

"I *do* go alone, but . . ."

"You have to be more independent, Valerie."

"I *am,*" she whined, grasping my hand. "I *love* being independent . . . but I *hate* being on my own."

I laughed.

"Everyone is asking, 'Where's Pete? Where's Pete?' and I never know what to say. I tell them, 'He's in his basement beating up a bag.' "

It was true. Sometimes I used boxing to avoid people. I worked out instead of going to parties. I did roadwork instead of going to dances.

"Partying is a waste of time," I said.

"Since when don't you like parties?"

"All you do is get drunk and high. I got to train. I got to win this thing."

"Aren't you ever lonely?" asked Valerie.

"Lonely? . . . sometimes," I said. "But I've got to get this boxing thing out of my system first."

"You make it sound like it's a disease or sickness."

"I'm not sick, I have a dream," I said, thinking about Tom.

"Some dream, Pete. You sound neurotic, if you ask me."

I shrugged. Valerie couldn't understand that having opponents who wanted to bust up your intestines was very time-consuming. I guess they had a tendency, like she said, to make me neurotic. But boxing, I felt, was one of the healthier neuroses in life.

"Do people really ask about me?" I asked.

"Yes," she said.

"What do they say?"

"They like you. You told me once yourself—you used to be 'Most Popular,' remember? People *like* you."

"That was a long time ago," I said. But still, I felt a glimmer of old happiness. I just wished that it didn't make me feel so vulnerable. For whatever reason, I knew that I was the sort of guy whom happiness harmed. I guess that's neurotic.

"I don't fit in with those people anymore," I said. "I'm not who they think I am."

"Of course you are," said Valerie. "Don't you realize that tonight two hundred kids from our school are coming to watch you fight?"

"Really?"

"That's three buses! You sold $1,600 worth of tickets!"

I wondered who all these people were. They couldn't really give a damn about me. I was only a media event for them. They were only a bunch of high school suburban kids slumming it for the night in New York City. That's all.

"I guess I'd better win, huh?"

"It would be a splendid idea," Valerie said, smiling.

"I'll give it my best shot," I said, shrugging my shoulders.

"You know what would be another splendid idea?" asked Valerie, sitting on my lap and running her fingers through my hair.

"What?"

"If you made love to me."

"Stop it," I said.

"Do you realize that you're the person who introduced me to the smell of male semen?" she said, giggling.

"Knock it off."

"Why?" she mewed softly, licking my earlobe.

"Because I'm just a dumb fighter."

"Ooo-h, I love dumb fighters," she said, stroking my thigh.

"I'll rip your guts out if you give me the chance," I warned.

"Oh, would you, please?" she begged. "That's what I came here for."

I laughed.

"Let's do something naughty," she said.

I shook my head and wondered what her father, Mr. Clinton, a serious Wall Street analyst, would have thought if he could hear his daughter.

"Let's go into your bedroom right now and do something absolutely hard core and X-rated," she said. She parted her legs, pushed out her breasts and pursed her lips like a slut.

"I don't want to hurt your feelings, Valerie," I said, "but I'm feeling so unromantic right now that I'm looking at your tits—and I know they're great—but they look like bags of meat."

She laughed and whined at the same time. "Well, I guess it's difficult to feel sexy when you know someone wants to bust up your intestines."

"And alter my pretty face," I added.

Fight time was approaching, and I found myself wishing that Valerie and I could stay safe in the kitchen forever. That's why I had to finally throw her out of the house.

I had to dodge intimacy with as much skill as I dodged punches in the ring. Intimacy was dangerous. Intimacy was chocolate donuts.

I had to be tough. I had to rely only on myself—not Valerie, not two hundred fans, not my family, not anybody. Only me. That's what boxing was all about.

At 4:10, I opened the heavy oak door of the Reformed Protestant Church, walked halfway down the aisle and sat down in one of the hard wooden pews. Before all my fights, I prayed at either the Protestant Church or Temple Beth El. With each fight, I alternated. I assumed the same God was listening.

I had never been particularly religious but something about boxing made me church-bound.

I started to pray my usual, homemade prayer. But, again, it

was only words. Words are hollow. They never fit what you try to say.

Twenty-four years ago, in this very church, my mother had said "I do" to my father. Those words were hollow, too. Sometimes I felt that people would be better off if they were born with no mouth.

I hoped my prayer was different. Like Huckleberry Finn said: "You can't pray a lie."

". . . and Dear God, about my fight tonight, please help me to fight my best. I'm not asking for victory. Please look over me, and my opponent, so no one really gets injured. Please bless me and walk with me. Please strengthen me, dear God, Amen."

For some reason, I wanted to cry, but I pretended I was on that TV screen so I wouldn't. I bowed my head and attempted to talk to God again. I wanted to tell him how I felt—like a potent seedling in contaminated soil. But I couldn't explain my life to God, Valerie or my parents, any more than I could explain it to myself. I was unintelligible.

And this boxing was crazy. It was stupid, self-inflicted suffering. Why was I doing it?

The tip—the tip of the tip—of my consciousness felt a mental nudging inside of me. There was a different person, alive, pulsating, kicking, beneath my own skin. A person I didn't know. Someone I had never met . . .

PETER: Can't you see that your stepfather has seeped into you?

ME: No way.

PETER: You're becoming exactly what you hate. You're becoming him.

ME: That's a lie!

PETER: You're both fighters.

ME: No! We're completely different.

PETER: Then why are you fighting?

ME: To prove a guy like me can be just as tough as a douche like him.

PETER: A guy like you?

ME: Leave me alone.

PETER: What do you mean, 'a guy like you'?

ME: Are you trying to open me up or something?

PETER: I just want to understand you.

ME: . . . a guy like my father, okay?

PETER: What does that mean?

ME: . . .

I stood up quickly and slid out of the pew. Swiveling my neck like a fighter, I stamped out of the church.

Outside, a woman was sitting on a bench in front of the church. She was wearing an expensive mink coat and a matching hat. I wondered if she realized that she was wearing dead animals. Probably not, if she was anything like my mother. With her sat a small boy swinging his short legs. The woman was licking a huge orange-green-blue-red lollipop. It seemed odd, but you never can understand these pseudo-sophisticated geeks. They're a different breed. And, of course, she didn't even look up until I slammed the church door. She wiped her tongue on the lollipop one more time and handed it to the boy. So that, at least, explained the lollipop. Then she patted her sticky lips on her handkerchief and gazed at me as I walked past. I noticed that she had that same snooty look as my mother. You'd think she'd never seen a guy cry before.

Whisking away tears, I hurried toward town. I had an apple and a candy bar on my mind.

Apple and candy bar, apple and candy bar, apple . . .

It was then that I began thinking about my father. I was vaguely aware that sometimes I was ashamed of him. And I was ashamed that I was ashamed. He was so gentle and so soft spoken. He was, somehow, different from other fathers. He was born in England, and he never learned to play football or baseball. And he threw a ball like a girl. He embarrassed me a lot.

I remembered the time, years ago, when he told me about Jack Booth.

"When I was a young boy, about thirteen," said my father,

with his crisp English accent, "there was this bully boy named Jack Booth. Everyone was frightened of him."

"But not you, right, Daddy?" I asked, hopefully.

"Including me," he said. "He was so much bigger than everyone else. And he was mean. Well, every day after school, I would walk home through a meadow. It was a beautiful meadow with rolling hills and wildflowers. And I would always be sure to pick some of the flowers for my mum. Daffodils, black-eyed Susans, daisies. One day, big Jack Booth was there, sitting on the fence. He saw me and called out, 'Hey! What're you doin'?' I told him, 'Picking flowers.' 'Fer who?' he asked. 'My mum,' I said. 'What a bleedin' sissy!' he scoffed."

"You weren't scared then, were you, Daddy?" I asked.

"Yes, I was, but I ignored him, and I kept picking flowers. Then he hopped down from his fence and approached me. 'You're a bleedin' sissy,' he repeated. Then he grabbed my flowers and threw them to the ground. The next thing I knew, I was sitting on top of his chest walloping his face with my fists."

"Hooray!" I cried. The picture of my father beating up a bully was, somehow, very pleasing. "I bet he didn't bother you after that, right, Dad?"

My father looked into the air as if seeing the past. "No, he didn't. In fact, he wanted very much to be my friend."

"That's me," I said to myself softly. I entered the supermarket to buy my apple and candy bar and repeated, "That's me. That's me. That's me . . ."

NINE

THE QUARTERFINALS

White Trash

"Ready, son?" asked Tom. His white fish-eye stared from his face like a dead pulpy marble.

I nodded my head.

"Okay, let's do it." Tom swung open the service entrance door of the Felt Forum and we walked in.

"Watt's here," declared Tom smartly.

The gray-haired geezer sitting behind the reception desk looked at us and was not impressed. He was wearing his red jacket with the gold Madison Square Garden emblem on the breast. He smoked a Marlboro.

"Cards," he said flatly.

"Cards?" said Tom. "Why cards? You remember us. This is Watt—the middleweight champ."

"Cards," repeated the official tiredly.

"In a coupla years," sniffed Tom, handing the official our A.A.U. registration cards, "you're gonna be asking' us for autographs, not no rinky dinky cards."

"He's not champ yet," observed the official

* * *

"Look, cameras," said Tom, pointing with his chin. We walked down the corridor. I noticed "ABC SPORTS" decaled to the side of a camera.

"Kid," beamed Tom, "you're gonna be on TV."

After winning four bouts in one month, I could balance my face okay, but I couldn't yet, balance my brain. Boxing on national television was scary. America would be watching me in its living rooms. This was getting too damn serious. This was the New York Golden Gloves Quarterfinals, the time when the guys with fragile minds get weeded out. It wasn't just a high school kid filming me anymore.

An ABC correspondent was interviewing a Puerto Rican boxer who was flashing his Golden Glove necklaces. They were standing in a puddle of bright floodlights and jamming up the narrow hallway. I tipped my black porkpie hat over my eyes and leaned against the green wall. Next to me loitered two former fighters, now trainers, both wearing green P.A.L. cardigan sweaters. I listened to their blurred conversation. Their thick, smudged sentences were about the upcoming Ali-Frazier championship fight.

I tried to ignore everyone and everything by slipping my mind into a mellow neutral. I stared at my sneakers and thought about not thinking. In a few seconds I was thinking about me thinking about not thinking. I spit onto the concrete floor. I tried to envision what nothingness inside an emptiness would look like. I listened to my breath go in and out.

Tom and I finally entered one of the many dressing rooms along the corridor.

"You ain't got no heavyweights, do you?" asked a fat guy rising from a wooden bench. "I don't want no meatball heavyweight in here with my boy."

"Middleweight," said Tom banging his bag on the floor, claiming territory. Then he began clearing away a spot for me to undress. "Get ready," ordered Tom, ignoring the fat man's stare.

"Middleweight's okay," acquiesced the obese trainer. As he sat down, the bench groaned beneath his tremendous weight. "I don't like two heavies together, it's bad luck."

Out of the corner of my eye, I glimpsed the man. His body was buried in yellow human fat. His wobbly cheeks, or jowls, looked like small stomachs, and the flesh on his face appeared unwashed. On his left cheek was a large red boil with a white head. Surrounding it were black whisker nubs.

"Where you guys from?" he asked.

"Jersey City," offered Tom, rummaging around in his bag for tape.

"Nice place, Jersey City."

"If you're a rat," said Tom.

The blond heavyweight in the corner laughed.

His dumpy trainer guffawed and said, "We ain't from no paradise, either."

"Where's paradise?" asked Tom.

"It ain't on Avenue B in New York City!" laughed the fat man.

"Only thing wrong with New York City," said Tom, "is that it's **in** New York City."

"Fuckin'-A," agreed the heavyweight.

"Got plenty of rats here, too," said his trainer.

"That's nothing that a rise in the ocean level wouldn't cure," quipped Tom.

The two laughed good-naturedly.

I began stripping off my red flannel lumberjack shirt. I felt a sense of drawing together, a camaraderie. But I fought against it. It wasn't part of my plan. I pulled off my two t-shirts. I wore two because it made me look bigger.

"Name's O'Conner," said the fat man, offering his hand to Tom, "but most people call me 'the Big-O.' "

"Hi," said Tom.

"And this here's Johnny Cap—the best heavyweight in this

tournament. He'll take the head off your shoulders with that right hand of his."

The heavyweight covered his college-boy face with his huge hands and shook his head with embarrassment.

"I didn't get your name, pal," said Big-O.

"Name's Brandy."

"Pete Watt," I said, putting on a smile.

"Watt . . . I think I seen your picture in the *News,*" said the heavyweight.

"Twice on the back page," bragged Tom.

"Yeah, that's right," said the heavyweight, smiling. "I remember now. You knocked some dude clear out of the ring. Whoooosh!"

I smiled.

Big-O cocked an eyebrow. "What kind of style you got, kid?"

"Early rudimentary," joked Tom, clapping my back. "This kid's got the furriest animal in him you ever saw."

I smiled softly. I hated to admit it, but I needed Tom to say this. I needed to hear that I was good and had talent. It was the same with my football coach at school. But their attention scared me. It put on pressure. It was like I had to reach their expectations. If I didn't, I'd be a disappointment, a failure and a bum. But I knew that I'd be stronger if I accepted Tom's praise rather than run from it. I didn't want the furry animal in me to be a bunny rabbit.

I did every little obsessive thing to win. I clipped my fingernails short to make my hands weigh less so I could punch quicker. I cut my hair short so if I got punched, my hair wouldn't fly around making the punch look better than it was. I wore two t-shirts. I didn't chew gum or toothpicks; chewing took energy. There were a lot of small things—like feinting at telephone poles and hitting socks against the wall. I'd do anything to get an edge. I was going to do whatever compulsive thing it took to turn my bed-wetting, thumb-sucking self into a fighter. Maybe I was neurotic, like Valerie said.

"I won't let you down, Tom," I said, swiveling my neck and punching the air.

Tom smiled at me. "I know you won't, son."

When you're sitting in a dressing room before a fight, there's not many things to do for fun. Really. You can't joke around or eat food or watch television. Some fighters play cards. Some curl up into a quiet and despondent sleep. Everyone seeks protection from what scares them the most—a knockout, a snapped tooth or quitting. Blacks listened to soul. Puerto Ricans escaped into salsa. Us whites were forced to listen to both. Me? I slept. And burped. And for some reason I smelled my hands. There was always a faintly weird smell on my palms, even between the fingers and on the webs. Maybe it was mildew or fungus from inside the gym's boxing gloves. You never knew what grew in them. I wouldn't call smelling my hands fun, but it was something to do.

"Something wrong with your nose, boy?" asked Big-O, eyeing me.

"Football injury," I lied, wiggling the cartilage in my nose.

"Cap here plays football, too," said Big-O.

"Defensive end," volunteered the heavyweight.

"Huh," I said, shaking my head. I looked at his physique. He was wearing only a jock. His body looked very well formed. He had that chiseled look that only a few football players get.

Suddenly, his rear end coughed up a fantastic fart. It ricocheted off the hard wooden bench.

"That's what I call a heavyweight fart," chirped Tom.

"That coulda filled a damn balloon! I told you to stop doin' that!" yelled Big-O angrily.

"I didn't do it! Honest!" laughed the heavyweight. "It was a tree frog!"

"You're the biggest tree frog I ever saw, you fartin' son of a bitch!" said Big-O as he dabbed with his sleeve at the pus drooling from his boil. "Look, you better start getting ready."

"We got plenty of time," said Cap.

"Do as I say. I want you ready now."

Cap stood slowly and began shadowboxing against the concrete wall. He looked good. There was snap in his punches, and his balance was correct. I noticed a tattoo on the right cheek of his ass. It said:

"U.S. PRIME CUT, #1 CHOICE, GRADE A BEEF."

When you haven't anything to do but stare at a tattooed ass, you remember things in spite of yourself. My brother, Dan, had a tattoo. I got a damp feeling remembering the first time I saw it. It was when I had barged into our bathroom at home. There was so much steam inside that I could almost chew it. Through the white fuzz I saw Dan. He was slumped over, asleep on the toilet bowl. I walked closer to wake him. That's when I saw his tattoo. My knees buckled, and I almost fainted. On his arm was a red heart and in it were the words: MOM AND DAD. That was the year my mother split up with my father.

Just thinking about Dan was like eating a raw piece of yesterday. That year he began talking about "cortex candy." I didn't know what it was; I was nine years old.

When Dan got older, he used to slip into my mother's purple dress and drive around town in her Cadillac while high on speed. When he was eighteen, he married a prostitute. True. A slut. Julie was a seventeen-year-old slut from our hometown. She turned tricks on weekends. Her father, a car salesman, told my father that she wasn't mature enough yet to get married because she still left her dirty underwear, with brown skid-marks, lying on her bedroom floor at home. Still, they got married. They spent their honeymoon ten miles away, in Greenwich Village. At three o'clock in the morning on their wedding night they were driving down Houston Street in my mother's red Cadillac. They ran a red light and plowed into a bread truck. They were high on smack. Julie's two front teeth were knocked out. Dan's jaw was fractured in three places. Nice honeymoon.

Five months later, Julie walked into the bathroom in their apartment and found Dan lying on the floor next to the toilet bowl. A needle was stuck in his vein. An ambulance rushed him to the hospital and he was pronounced D.O.A. Somehow, though, the doctors got his heart pumping again.

Even though he was a lousy hunk of junk and we didn't get along too well, I didn't want to lose my only brother. I loved him. I remember I once threw a meatball into his right ear because I caught him stealing twenty dollars from the money box hidden in the back of my sock drawer. I figure, now, it was the drugs.

He wasn't always a screwball, Dan. I personally think it was the Ceffone influence. He took it bad. Still in all, just thinking about him is pretty raw.

My mother liked to brag to the people at her country club that Dan and I were two of the finest "cherubs" in the world. It was the tone in her saccharine, cultured voice that I hated most. She was always pretending everybody was fine.

But Dan's mind must have been a mangled mess of mush. Like mine. He had cortex candy. I had boxing. He had a monkey on his back, I developed one in my head. Same difference.

But I don't need him anymore. I'm my own brother. And I don't need my mother. Dan and I became niggers so she could be a princess.

I just wanted to sit alone where I could be quiet and hate them both. I gazed at the heavyweight. He was a fool; chewing a toothpick and wasting energy. I counted and recounted the coat hangers on the wall. There were twenty-seven . . . twenty-seven . . . twenty-seven . . .

Suddenly, the dressing room door yawned open. A head popped in. "Is Watt in here?"

I looked away from the coat hangers and saw that it was the reporter who had interviewed Tom and me after my last fight.

"Why ain't you at the horses?" snapped Tom.

"I wish I was," he answered. Then he gazed down at me and smiled. "How's life in Jersey City, Pete?"

I looked away from his knowing blue eyes.

"Hey!" said Tom angrily. "I gave you an interview last time, and I never saw it in the paper. Why not?"

"Sorry," shrugged the reporter. "You win some, you lose some."

"Don't give me that. Why not?"

"That boy, Americo Valero, gave me a better story."

"Oh, yeah? Well, then you'd better pack your bags and get outta here," Tom said, bristling.

"What bags?" asked the reporter.

"Those small ones between your legs," Tom said.

The reporter chuckled. "Well, actually, Brandy, I've got some bad news for you two."

My head swung around.

"Bad news?" asked Tom.

"Yup. You win some, you lose some."

Tom stood up. "Stop blabbin' and tell us what you're sayin'."

"They found out and disqualified us, Tom," I mumbled.

"Disqualified!" shouted Tom indignantly.

The reporter smiled. "No, not exactly. It's worse."

"Worse?" said Tom.

My heart pounded.

"I thought that I'd be the first to tell you. You're going to have one helluva fight tonight, gentlemen."

"Whatya mean?" asked Tom.

"You just drew the best fighter in your weight division."

Tom and I stared blankly at the reporter's grin.

"You're fighting Gillio."

The word "Gillio" tore into my cerebrum like a sharp splinter. The Navy champ.

"That's life in the big city, kid," observed Big-O, dabbing at his boil.

"I want a clean fight, no rabbit punches . . ."

Five inches away, Mike "The Brooklyn Bomber" Gillio glared at me. The arrogant sneer on his face pissed me off. It was a damn risky look for a guy to be wearing in public; it meant something was going to happen very shortly.

". . . if someone gets knocked down, I want the fighter standing to go to the farthest neutral corner . . ."

Gillio's blue eyes snapped like firecrackers, and his face was slick with sweat. His blond hair was Vaselined in a smooth smear across his forehead. It looked as though it had been painted onto his scalp with a paint brush.

". . . and I don't want no rough stuff. This is for television and if I . . ."

Gillio was Italian, but as I stared him in the eyes, I knew there was Kraut in him somewhere. He resembled a German shepherd dog, one that doesn't bark, but just sits there waiting to pounce.

". . . and I'm not going to tell you twice about hittin' low. Is that understood?"

Gillio and I scowled at each other silently.

"Do you understand, boys?" repeated the referee.

"Yeah," said Gillio's handler.

"Shake hands and come out fighting."

No one shook hands.

CLANG!

Gillio waded into me, winging wicked lefts and rights. He caught me on the neck and shoulders but not my face. Rather than back up, I crouched down low—much lower than usual. It was the safest place, next to his baby-blue trunks. I set myself and was about to leap up with a left to smash in his arrogant puss, but he grabbed my arms and forced a clinch.

Fear flashed in my mind. This guy was powerful. It had never been necessary for me to crouch so low to escape punishment. We were about the same size but he was broader, thicker and older. Clinching with him was like grabbing onto a slithery human bicep.

The ref finally untied us.

Gillio stalked me. Like a typical military boxer, he only knew forward. I triple jabbed, backing up. All three missed. He leaned forward stiffly, like all the military boxers do, and burrowed in with both hands. I almost swallowed his left fist as it crashed into my mouth. A right smashed into my nose, and sucking back tears, I clinched. I could smell the odor of his strength oozing from his pores. This guy came to fight!

The ref broke us but Gillio was on me again, flailing with lefts and rights. I had to start doing something quickly—there are no runners-up in a prize fight.

I danced away and jabbed. Gillio chased. He didn't respect jabs; he walked into them. I decided to do what I had told myself to do while lying safely in bed three nights ago. It was strategy for a slugger. I danced back quickly. Gillio followed. Suddenly, I stepped in and shot a straight right hand. CRACK! It caught him off balance. I planted my feet and flung in a left hook. SMACK! It plopped onto his jaw. Burns, Compo and Green all went down with the identical punch, but Gillio went berserk.

He charged and trapped me in the corner. Shots slammed into my sides, arms and gloves. I tried to clinch but he pushed me away. I ducked and weaved. His punches exploded into me. For the first time, I heard the screaming crowd. I must have looked hurt. They were going nuts.

Finally, I was able to clinch. I noticed, on Gillio's chest, a few splurts of blood. Somebody was bleeding. As the referee parted us, he peered into my eyes to see if I was okay. I was fine. In fact, I smiled at Gillio. It was then that I saw who was bleeding—Gillio.

The bell rang.

Tom slapped me hard on the cheek. "You're a piece of white trash, ya know that?"

I looked up at his angry face. His knitted eyebrows and crazed expression reminded me of my stepfather's. Like a child, I felt a pang of fear.

"I'm sorry," I said.

Tom slapped me again. "There's no sorry to it! If I knew you was white trash, I wouldn't have bothered with ya! How many times do I gotta tell ya not to back up?"

"Sorry," I gasped.

"I want lateral movement, you hear me?"

"Yes."

"Okay, now breathe." Tom held the elastic waist of my cup and trunks as I gulped in cigarette-gray air. Already I was tired. My heart thudded in my chest. Asthma sucks. Breathing deeply on my stool, I remembered going to the fights with my father as a kid. I watched the crowds and secretly thought: Someday I'm going to be the fighter, and someday you'll all be watching me in the ring. I'm going to show you all how it's done. Someday.

The ten-second buzzer sounded—time enough for three deep breaths.

CLANG!

Gillio charged. I jammed three jabs into his face; he ate all three. He countered with a right hand. I sidestepped to his left, and it bulleted past my ear. Tom was right—lateral movement was the key. Military fighters are programmed automatons that can't handle movement. They're made from the same cookie cutter. They're basic and simple—search and destroy. To them, movement was cowardly guerrilla warfare.

But not Gillio. He began cutting the ring on me. He slammed a four-punch combo into my gut. I gasped and held on. Only an experienced fighter can cut a ring effectively. And Gillio was doing it.

From then on, the fight was as scientific as a spear. When you're trapped, you go crazy. You break. I began bludgeoning at his face with lefts and rights. No strategy. No nothing. I loaded up with each shot and tried to take him out. I was hitting him in the face and stomach like he was a damn sandbag. He was slugging at me like a machine. When I missed my left hook, I swerved my torso around and came up with it again and again and again. THUD! THUD! THUD!

Suddenly, he caught me with his best punch. It exploded on my nose. I heard a sickening sound of crunching gristle. It sounded like a chicken drumstick being torn from its socket. It sounded like a busted nose. White trash.

I ripped in punches nonstop. Not at his head—through it. I bombed his Kraut face. For the first time in the fight, he backed up. Like a dog, I almost bit his shoulder. Our close-quarters battle was brutal, if not pretty. Blood was flying. Two vicious mammals were maiming each other, and the yelling crowd was appreciating it. They were cheering their brains out.

The bell rang.

Dead tired, I slumped on my stool. Each breath was a labored, rasping groan. My nose was bleeding like a fountain.

"Relax—relax—you're in a fight—you're in a fight," said Tom worriedly. "Breathe! Breathe!"

I tried to fill my lungs with oxygen, but that gray stuff wasn't much better than carbon monoxide. I could see me watching myself gasping for air. I looked tired. I was tired. Real tired.

"Everything's copacetic," said Tom, digging into his hip pocket. He brought out the bottle and held it to my lips. "Drink!"

I gulped it down sloppily.

"Listen, son—you took that round. I need one more. You got it in ya?" asked Tom, swabbing out my nostrils with a Q-tip.

I blinked my eyes "yes" even though my heart and lungs were screaming.

"Listen—you ain't tired! You can take this guy. You're sparrin' with Hopkins, and Hopkins sparred with Sonny Liston!"

Tom was grasping for logic like I was for air.

"You can do it!"

Bloody snot hung from the tip of my nose. I had dreamed of battles all my life. I recalled my thrilling childhood visions of broken-nosed glory and flat-nosed manhood. I had wanted this. But as I sat on my blood-soaked stool rasping for air, I realized that it was all a magnificent illusion. Fighting is delightful only to those who have no experience of it.

The ten-second buzzer sounded.

"Pete! Look for the glass in his eyes. Finish him off!" shouted Tom, hunching between the ropes.

CLANG!

We met center ring and plugged. Don't give me this shit about blood clots or anything—I didn't care. Neither did he. His cocky German face looked like raw meat. Till that time, I had never hit a guy harder. Sure, I was getting nailed, too, with lefts and rights. It was hard to tell my slamming heartbeat from his punches. But what the fuck . . . I got this far, I refused to lie down or quit. My mind was in a moonlit area beyond scared.

By the middle of the round, I had thrown, and landed, so many left hooks, I couldn't hold up my left arm anymore. It dangled by my side. I had to rely upon my right. But I could tell that Gillio was still leery about my left hook. So I feinted with my left shoulder and fired a right uppercut. It smashed onto his jawbone. Hurt, he grabbed for my arms and clinched. He leaned in and put his damaged nose, with all the blood coming out of it, on my mouth. It tasted like blood, all right, and sweat.

I pushed him off with my shoulders and tried to finish him. But military guys, if nothing more, have endurance. Gillio was no different. He battered me with all he had.

I felt ninety-eight percent dead. But a thick-skinned stupidity kept me going. I dug down deep and tried to coax out the furry figure who swung from branch to branch in the back of my brain. But by now, my punches were limp bullets. My ribs heaved with exhaustion. Flesh burned away, melting in hot sweat drops. Punching nonstop, I was a piece of perfect rage. Cortex candy.

Dear God, I begged—help me!—help me! I clawed down deeper and I was able to drag one more exhausted and desperate fist through the smoky air. It smacked onto his bloody face.

Down he went!

Clang!

I watched Gillio pick himself off the canvas. His blue eyes weren't snapping anymore. But he looked at me and smiled. We embraced warmly. Blood matted his face and chest. Blood streamed from my nose.

"Good fight," he panted.

"Goofigh," I gasped.

I don't give a damn if it sounds corny, but that's the beauty of boxing; a rugged three-round fight makes two very different people very much the same.

I left the ring before the decision because I knew I was going to puke. I knew it was close, but I hoped that my knockdown would make the difference.

I almost fainted as I walked to my dressing room. I had to sit down twice before I finally made it. Once I entered, I began dry heaving. "AAWWH! AAWWH! AAWWH!" I doubled myself up on the bench in agony.

"GEESH! That musta been some fight!" exclaimed Big-O. "You okay?"

"He's fine," said Tom. "Here—wet this towel for me."

"AAWWH! AAWWH!"

Tom draped the cool towel around my neck and sponged down my face. It felt good.

"Relax, Pete. It's okay," he whispered.

"You want a doctor?" asked Big-O.

I raised my head. "I don't need . . . AAWWH!"

"No doctor," said Tom.

The door opened and someone yelled, "CONGRATS, WATT, YOU WON!"

"AAWWH!"

"Shit! Is he okay?" asked the voice.

"Dehydration," said Tom.

I looked up and saw Johnny Cap, the heavyweight, leaning in at a forward angle gawking at me. Then he glanced at the door as if he might still be able to jump out of it and run back home.

"Our turn, Cap," said Big-O, standing up slowly.

"Do it up!" said Tom, kneading my neck.

Ten minutes later, I felt strong enough to stand.

Tom looked at me strangely and said, "The thing I said before . . . I didn't mean it."

"What's that?"

"I called you . . . white trash."

"No problem," I said, shuffling slowly to the sink for a drink.

"I hated to say it," said Tom, shaking his head forlornly. "I never thought I'd say those damn words."

"I don't care," I said, touching the cool stream of water flowing from the tap.

"That's what my stepfather used to call me—white trash. 'Come here, you white trash!' I hated it when he called me that. But, ya know, it always got me going."

Tom shook his head again. "You treat a guy like dirt, and he'll grow flowers."

I stared at Tom from the porcelain sink.

"I hated that man's guts, and now I'm actin' like him," lamented Tom.

"It's okay," I said.

"No, it ain't okay!" shouted Tom. "I can't shake the fuckin' man. I see him every goddamn time I look in the goddamn mirror. And now I'm even talkin' like him." Tom grinned hideously at me, and the crevices in his cheeks changed direction. "When I die, I want to be cremated and have my ashes thrown in my stepfather's fuckin' face!" His mouth slammed shut like a car door. He then walked up to the mirror and slammed it with his hands. "Who do ya think mutilated my eye?"

"Canzoneri," I said.

"Canzoneri, shit!" said Tom. "That was all a lie. I sparred Canzoneri only five or six times—that's it. The old man did it. That's who. With a shovel. So now I see everything with one eye. You understand? One fuckin' eye. And I gotta see *him* each time I look in the damn mirror. Understand?"

I nodded my head.

It was as if a black plug had been pulled from the basement of my soul and I could look down deep into myself with a flashlight. And I liked what I saw down there.

I stood in front of the mirror and combed my hair. I noticed that I could see my mother's face in mine. I thought about Tom and realized for the first time that I'm not just only me.

"That reporter was right," said Tom, entering the bathroom.

"What's that?" I asked.

"Gillio was tough—tougher than anybody else you fought so far."

"You ain't kidding," I said, sighing.

"You understand, don't ya, what that makes *you* now?"

"What?" I asked, looking at my mother in the mirror.

"The *toughest!*" he said, patting me on the head like a kitten. I shrugged.

"Hey," said Tom, "how about you and me gettin' a hamburger and a beer?"

My stomach imagined a hamburger and a beer.

"I'm not too hungry, but I wouldn't mind a chocolate donut," I said.

TEN

THE SCHOOL

Wiggles

The alarm clock spanked the early morning air. I creaked open my eyes and a yellow crumb of sleep fell onto the pillow. I was jolted back into consciousness—from the there into the here. But it wasn't hard to wake. I had been having a recurring nightmare about the roller coaster.

My head, one big bruise on the pillow, throbbed like a bad tooth. The flesh was black and purple under both eyes and on the bridge of my nose. But the worst was not being able to open my mouth because my jaw muscles were battered raw. I remembered when black eyes were something to brag about. Trophies. Maybe I'll end up looking like Jack Palance after all, I thought.

My mother stood in the doorway and gazed at me. A hand was pressed to her lips. "Oh, sweetie. Look at your face." Her voice had its usual sugary tone, and her moist eyes showed motherly concern.

I wanted to smack her. I remembered when she was my mother and I loved her—now she was Ceffone's wife and I hated her.

"Are you all right, kitten? Do you hurt?" she asked.

"No," I said.

She walked to the right side of my bed with short, tense, immaculate steps and sat down. I looked at her full-length mink and Fifth Avenue suit. I smelled her expensive French perfume. Her hair looked like spun glass. She made me feel shamefully rich, and I wanted the guys at the gym to know that I had nothing to do with her.

She raised a hand and tried to touch my right eye.

"Don't pet me!" I didn't say it loudly, but I said it into her face. It was a pretty face—I had to admit that. But I realized an important fact: pretty mothers make shitty mothers.

She stiffened and backed off. "Look at you. Reminds me of when you were a baby."

"What do you mean?"

"When you and your brother Dan were little I used to spend so much time running after you making sure you didn't fall off your bike or burn yourself with matches or hit your head against the table corner . . ."

"Uh-huh."

"And now look at you. I spent all that time so a stranger can knock you on the head for fun."

I smiled despite myself. "I won," I said proudly. But somewhere I felt a vague danger and I looked away.

"Yes, I know," she nodded.

"The youth of today stink, don't they?" I said.

"Don't be a smart-mouth," she said. She sounded like my stepfather.

"Then don't mother me," I said.

"I am your mother."

"Yeah, I know," I said, still avoiding her eyes.

She stood and high-heeled noisily to the door.

I sneezed.

She turned. "Catching something?"

"No," I said, looking at the bloody egg yolk of snot in my hand.

"Well, be careful, sweetie. I've got to run, I'm late. If you want, there's an ice pack in the fridge. Bye!"

"Mom?" I said quickly.

She turned. "Yes?"

"How come you divorced my father?" I said it.

She stiffened.

"How come you left Dad?"

She walked slowly back into the room and sat down on my bed. Her expression was suddenly motherly. It made me sick. She reached out to rub my leg, but I moved it away. "Dear," she explained, "your father and I fell out of love."

"You left *him*," I corrected.

"Yes," she admitted, "that's true."

"Why?" I repeated.

She opened her mouth and out came a soft mothlike sound. "It was just one of those things, dear. It was no one's fault."

"Why did you leave him?" I repeated.

"Oh, Peter," she said, closing her eyes and rubbing her temples with her fingers, "it's too early in the morning for this. Don't ask me these questions."

"Why not?"

"It's so complicated, dear. You wouldn't understand."

"Tell me. Why?" I pressed.

She sighed deeply. "Your father is a fine man, but there came a time when we couldn't live together."

We sat silently and stared over each other's shoulders. She still hadn't answered my question. Suddenly I said, "You left him because you thought he was too nice, didn't you?"

"Too nice? What do you mean?"

"He wasn't mean enough."

She tilted her head.

I had heard of people like that—the more you beat them, the more they respected you. I wondered if my mother was that type—beat her and she'll love you. I knew Ceffone slapped her around when he was drunk. "You thought he was too . . . gentle," I said.

"Too gentle?"

"Yeah."

"That's silly," she said, giving a nervous laugh.

"Ceffone slaps you."

"Never!" she exclaimed, tensing up again.

"When you lost your diamond bracelet, remember?"

"That's nonsense."

"And last week, after your bridge game, outside on the patio."

"That's not your concern," she snapped, icing over.

"It *is* my concern."

"When I want your help, I'll ask you for it."

She suddenly looked away, over my shoulder, away, and was silent. I looked at her face. I guess she *was* that type.

"So, you didn't think he was . . . masculine," I said.

"Who?"

"My father."

"Your father was very masculine."

"Was?"

"Is," she corrected.

"Not like Ceffone," I said.

"No, not like Mr. Ceffone."

Mentally, I pictured Ceffone and my father in the street fist-fighting: a big, confident, quick-witted lawyer pitted against a nice Jew songwriter—who once bought flowers for someone lying in a hospital bed. No contest.

"Your father is an artist," said my mother. "He's sensitive."

"Yeah."

"And your stepfather is . . ."

"Insensitive."

"No," she said, "different."

"How could you marry someone so *different?*"

She sighed. "Your stepfather is generous."

"When he's not slapping you, or . . ." I didn't say "stabbing you."

Again, she stiffened. She knew. "Look around you," she said

defensively. "He's an excellent provider, Peter. And don't you forget it."

"That's *why* you left my father?" I repeated.

Out came that moth sound.

"You don't want to answer me," I said.

"Why wouldn't I?"

"I don't know," I said. "Maybe you're ashamed."

"Of whom?"

"Yourself."

She blinked.

"I know why you left him," I said.

"Oh?"

"You don't want to tell me, but I know."

She looked into my eyes.

"He wasn't writing any more hit songs."

"That's utter nonsense."

"You dumped him."

She stood up indignantly.

"He was sinking and you walked out."

"You always did love him more than you loved me," she said.

"You dumped him—for money."

"Is that what you *really* think?"

"Yeah."

"Not true."

"Bucks. Look around you."

She went to slap my mouth, but missed.

"You got what you wanted—Europe, the country club, the maid, your Cadillac, your number '1' license plate . . ."

"Peter!"

"Dan and I go through *hell* for you. Dan's a junkie 'cause of *you*. It's *your* fault!"

"We'll talk about this later!" she said as she fled from the room.

I yelled at her back, "and you're right—my father *is* different—he doesn't stab people!"

She swung around. "We'll discuss this," she said, quivering, "when I get home."

"Home? . . . nuthouse!" I shouted.

"Be thankful for what you have," she murmured as she strode out of the room to the comfort of her red Cadillac. She loved that car.

Quickly I shut my eyes before she turned her back on me. I concentrated again on my nightmare . . . My stepfather and I sat in a roller coaster. Just sitting next to him angered me. I could hear the clackety-clack as it slowly climbed. I stood up and slugged him. He looked at me and smiled. The harder I punched, the louder he laughed. I always woke up with him still laughing.

"Holy cow! Look at your face!"

"You sound like my old lady," I said.

"Old lady?"

"My mother."

"Oh! That old lady."

I smiled. Mr. Goldsmith, my guidance counselor, was okay. "You see my fight last night?" I asked.

"Yep!"

"How did I look?"

"Tough as crabgrass," he said. He rocked back in his chair and clasped his hands behind his head.

I looked at his plastic nameplate on his desk. It read: Charles "Chuck" Goldsmith.

"The more I know you, Peter, the less I really know you," he said.

"What's that mean?" I said.

He looked into my eyes.

I began picking at the dry cuticle on my left index finger.

"I remember you as a skinny little freshman four years ago. You came in here nervous, shy and stuttering. Remember?"

I nodded my head.

"And then last night, I'm watching the same nervous, shy,

stuttering kid—but this time he's punching someone's lights out in the ring. I mean, who's this strange person who's Peter Watt?"

I laughed, not knowing what to say.

He looked at me and waited for an answer.

"People change," I said.

"Yes, that's true. And you've covered a lot of ground in four years. And in the future I hope you'll cover more."

"You mean I'm not always going to be this dumb jock?" I joked.

"Who knows?" he said, not smiling.

I looked away.

"I hope you're not always going to be a boxer. You can't buy a face, you know."

I thought about my mother. She was always talking about getting a face lift.

"What goes through your mind when you're hitting a guy?" asked Mr. Goldsmith.

"Last night it was, 'Oh, geez, I don't think I can hold on much longer.' I felt on the verge of being broken—especially in the third when my arms and legs and lungs were dead. So I guess I'm thinking 'Please, God, help me.' And I held on by a thread. Maybe that was the difference, that little thread."

"Determination," said Mr. Goldsmith, nodding his head.

I shrugged. On the wall I noticed a poster. It read:

> YOU BETTER NOT COMPROMISE YOURSELF.
> IT'S ALL YOU GOT.

"You taught a lot of high school students something about heart or guts or will, or another part of the anatomy," said Mr. Goldsmith, smiling.

"You mean balls?"

Mr. Goldsmith grinned. "As your guidance counselor, I can't say balls."

"Be serious, Mr. Goldsmith. I've heard you teachers in the teachers' room."

He smiled but suddenly stopped. "Something bothers me."

"What?"

"I see impurities," he said.

"Impurities?"

"When I was watching you last night, it reminded me of when I was six years old, the time I was looking in a microscope. I was looking at a slide of water, which I thought was clear and pure, and then I said to my father, 'Look! It has wiggles in it.' And he said, 'Yes, it's impure. You must look close.' And the truth of that water was that it was impure. And watching you last night, I think I saw wiggles."

I looked away and stared at his bookshelf. I saw *I'm O.K., You're O.K.* and *The Adolescent Mind* and *Analysis of Teenagers.*

"You know, people are like icebergs, Peter. Only the tip shows."

I thought I was calm but beneath the desk I found myself tearing into a hangnail.

"I think there might be wiggles in your motivation." He stared at me. "Are there?"

I tried to look him in the eyes, but the best I could do was his ear.

"Results—you won—big deal. Anyone can see results. The important ingredients are usually hidden. Roots of a tree, and all that stuff." He quietly waited for my response.

"It's fun," I said, breaking the silence.

"Boxing, fun?"

"Yeah, fun."

"That's ugly fun."

I listened to the music in the background, The Doors "Light My Fire." Goldsmith always had the radio playing. I was beginning to realize that he wasn't as cool as everyone believed. He was just trying to infiltrate.

"Boxing always struck me as the biggest symbolic act going. A fighter displaces and misplaces his anger." He leaned back in his chair. He thrummed his fingers on a gray filing cabinet. "Who are *you* angry at?"

"What are you talking about?"

"I think you know," he said. "It's important for you to realize that many actions are really unconscious reactions."

I squinted as warm blond sunlight plopped into the room.

"It's good to catch problems before they lump up and get beyond articulation. Otherwise, you wind up lying on a therapist's couch trying to untangle a convoluted head."

"You think my internal environment is polluted, huh?" I asked grinning.

Goldsmith laughed. "I didn't say that."

"Good. Because I don't have any problems."

"No?"

"No."

"I'm sure you don't need any pieces of wisdom from me, but everyone has problems."

"Well, I don't."

"Why, then, are you angry?"

"Who's angry?"

"I know when a kid's ticked."

"I'm different."

Mr. Goldsmith smiled. "You know what, Pete?"

I looked at him hard, like he was an opponent. "What?"

"You're full of shit."

I felt naked. I hated him. I guess I was angry.

"You're so emotionally blind it's pathetic. You can't even tell me why you box."

I scrambled around in my head for an answer. "It makes me feel good," I blurted.

"Yeah, yeah—it purifies the soul. I know all about it. Boxing provides an emotional laxative, a spiritual cleansing and all that crap—big deal. We know that—but from what?"

I could see what he was doing, and I wasn't going to fall for it. I picked up a yellow pencil and began doodling.

"You can't transfer your hate and resentment, Pete. You can't box and hit bags and people when there's something else bugging

you. It's no good, boxing. It's like yawning when you really want
to sneeze."

I kept silent and scribbled more, not wanting to give him an
opening. His stares penetrated me.

"Hello? . . . Hello in there?" he said. But I didn't fall for it.

He's jealous of me, I thought. I'm tougher than him and he
knows it. I can tough it out when he can't.

"You got to sneeze and get it out, Pete," he said.

"I don't gotta do nothin'," I said. He was trying to rob me of
my strength—my hate.

"Tough guy, huh?"

"That's right," I said. He's like the rest of them. They all want
you to be like them—loafers, short hair and pep rallies.

"I think this tough guy here is terrified," he said.

I looked up and spat, "Of what?" I could have bit my tongue
in two for taking his bait.

He tilted his head in appraisal. "I'm not sure. But I think
you're terrified of finding out what you already know."

What the hell is this guy talking about, I thought.

"Athletically you're boxing—emotionally you're crying. It's
obvious. What do you think of that?"

I doodled the word "therapist" quietly. I drew a line between
the "e" and the "r" so it looked like the/rapist. He wasn't going
to get any more out of me. He can dilute someone else—but not
me.

"Well, I have to hand it to you. I have a caseload of one
hundred and ten students, and out of all of them, you're the
toughest nut to crack. Well, I didn't call you in today to talk
about boxing or to get at the 'Peter-ness' of Peter. I want to talk
about college." He looked over some papers on his desk and said,
"S.A.T.'s aren't too bad—450 in math, 530 in English. I think
we can find a place for you." He looked up at me. "I'm assuming
that there's life after the New York Golden Gloves."

I felt anxious. Guys like Goldsmith were always making you
choose stuff.

"You know, one day you're going to wake up, and you're not going to feel like boxing anymore."

"How do you know?" I asked belligerently.

"Did you ever play with soldiers when you were a kid?"

"Yeah, so?"

"Do you remember the day you took them out to play with and you realized that you were too old for them?"

I nodded my head.

"It'll be the same with boxing. One day you'll want to hang 'em up. People molt."

"I don't want to talk about college right now," I said.

Goldsmith leaned back in his chair and said, "It never ceases to amaze me. People choose their professions with the same amount of forethought that they choose their socks in the morning."

"You sound like my mother," I said.

He leaned forward. "Oh?"

"Yeah, you both piss me off. Both of you think college is the answer for everything. The way I see it, a guy goes to college to learn to be an intelligent asshole."

"Really?" he said, taking off his glasses.

"Yeah. An asshole who becomes a snob at some country club and adjusts himself to the front page of the *Times* and the wonders of *Newsweek* magazine and the atomic bomb and gets fat on businessmen's lunches. Then he starts wearing a rag around his neck so everyone knows he's a man. Your world stinks."

"Those are interesting thoughts," said Goldsmith. "And what **is** a man?"

"If a man is what my stepfather is, then I don't want to be one."

"Your stepfather's not a man?"

"He's a college asshole who carries around a briefcase."

"Huh," said Goldsmith. "And what's in his briefcase?"

"His soul and his sandwich," I blurted.

Goldsmith sighed deeply. "Do you need to get your teeth

bashed in before you wake up and realize that boxing is no day at the beach, either? It's no way to be a man or to make a living. Boxing is a dog-eat-dog life."

"Screw you, Goldsmith!" I said, jumping up. "I know what you're doing."

"Oh?" he said, sipping calmly from a styrofoam coffee cup. "Tell me."

My mind scrambled for words. "You're trying to pry me open!" I blurted finally.

"Bingo!" he said.

Angrily I stamped down the corridor. I tried to pretend that there was no such person as Mr. Chuck Goldsmith, and if there was, I didn't know him. I didn't need someone nibbling and whittling away at me. Especially now. I wanted my mind blank and my motives muffled.

As I walked down the hall to math, I feinted and flinched like a fighter; I planned defenses and countered imaginary punches.

Coach Sgro passed me by the cafeteria. In college, Coach played defensive tackle under Vince Lombardi. I personally think that that experience caused him irreparable damage. He was not quite a sadist, but his heart was definitely a very dry bone. He did come up with good football teams, though.

Smiling, he gripped me by my neck and gave me his famous nut-cracker handshake. "Are you up for your next fight?" he asked.

"I think so."

"Think so? I didn't teach you 'Think so.'"

"I know so," I said, staring at his crew cut.

"That's better. When is it?"

"Next week," I said. I could feel his fat fingers slowly squeeze the back of my neck.

"I'll be there," he said.

I smiled, even though his fingers were embedding themselves deeper into my jugular. I realized that it was because of him—and maybe even Vince Lombardi—that I had made it this far.

"Don't forget your sprints," he warned.

"Okay."

"Excuse me?" he said, squeezing tighter.

"Yes, sir!"

Then he swung around and shoulder-blocked me into a locker. "Always be alert!" He smiled as he walked away.

I guess Coach didn't want me getting too confident.

The bell suddenly rang, and instantly the hallway was overflowing with mild madness. Youthful egos were darting about in adolescent confusion. Uncalm hormones. I looked at the pretty girls with budding breasts and wondered if they were ready for the big one.

I walked up one flight of noise to math. Whoever invented math should be shot; it's definitely a bad idea. I'm eighteen years old and I still count on my fingers sometimes. 8 + 5, 7 + 5 and 7 + 6 just haven't clicked yet. They still give me problems.

I sucked back a clot of phlegm and swallowed it down as I entered class.

"Golly! Look at your face," the teacher gasped, clutching his briefcase like an asshole.

ELEVEN

THE FAMILY

Dinner!

One evening after my three-mile roadwork (seven-minute miles with army boots), I sat at the dinner table eating supper: Haitian meatloaf, mashed potatoes and peas.

Only Rodney, Lance, Stacie, Lourdes (the maid) and I were home. Dan was out doing drugs, and Raquel was rehearsing for her debutante ball. Our parents were in Trenton, the state capital. My stepfather—because of political connections—had been nominated for state senator on the Republican ticket.

Rodney, eating, picked a small green pea from his plate and said, "Lance, know what this reminds me of?"

"What?" asked Lance, his mouth bulging full with meatloaf.

"Your brain," squeaked Rodney.

Lourdes smiled, not understanding English.

Lance picked up his own pea and rolled it in his palm. He sucked at his tooth, like his father. "Know what this reminds me of?" he lisped, effeminately. "Your testicle!"

Rodney threw down his napkin, pulled back his chair and blurted, "I'll get you for that!" He traipsed into the bathroom

163

and slammed the door shut. When he came back, he was holding something behind his back.

"What're you hiding?" asked Lance tensely.

"You'll find out," said Rodney, ambling forward.

Sensing chaos, I pulled away.

Rodney brought out his hand, and Lourdes gasped. He held a slice of toilet paper and on it was smeared a gooey chunk of light brown shit.

"Dinner!" hollered Rodney, reaching for Lance's face.

Lance recoiled, but not fast enough, and a brown skid of shit streaked down his cheek and neck.

"Get it off! Get it off!" screeched Lance.

Rodney dropped to the floor laughing.

Lance sprinted to the bathroom.

Lourdes held an apron to her mouth and heaved.

"You're rotten!" shouted Stacie, kicking Rodney's shoulder with her Hush-puppy.

Rodney contorted with laughter on the linoleum floor.

"Wait! . . . Wait! . . ." he gasped between peals of laughter.

"TU ANIMAL! TU ANIMAL!" screamed Lourdes, gagging at the sink.

"WAIT!" howled Rodney.

"MI DIOS! MI DIOS!" screamed Lourdes.

"I set you up!" gasped Rodney. "It was Skippy! Skippy peanut butter!"

Later that evening, Rodney was comfortably sprawled on a white leather couch. He was too absorbed with Matt Dillon and the bearded cattle-rustlers on "Gunsmoke" to notice Lance, or what he held—two wads of filthy toilet paper.

"Shake?" asked Lance, smiling.

Absorbed, Rodney offered his hand. Lance grabbed for it. Sensing something, Rodney pulled back.

"Get away!" shouted Rodney.

"What goes around, comes around," said Lance, coolly.

"Mine was a joke!"

"This is a joke, too!" explained Lance.

"You're gonna get it!" threatened Rodney.

"No, *you're* going to get it!" said Lance. Then he threw a wad at Rodney. It whapped wetly onto the white leather couch. Rodney sprinted out the front door. Lance chased, balancing a dirty wad in his hand.

Fifteen minutes later, they both walked back into the kitchen, scratched, bloodied and with shit smeared all over their faces.

"What happened?" I asked.

"None of your fuckin' business!" shot Rodney.

"Yeah, you don't even belong here!" yelled Lance.

"This is *our* house—not yours!" yelled Rodney.

No shit, I thought, coming very, very close to punching their shitty mouths. I could nail Rodney with a left hook; I could right cross Lance; I could spit in their faces; I could do a lot of things to make myself feel good. But something told me that I was already fighting on too many fronts.

Two nights later, after roadwork, I was resting on a couch—*another* couch. Suddenly I heard a car door slam. My flesh crawled. I jacked up and pretended to read a book. My stepfather was home.

I heard him at the door fumbling with his keys. He stumbled in. His hair was all messed up, and like always, he was smoking a cigar. But tonight the man was stinking drunk.

"There's the boxing-boy reading a book," he blurted.

I said nothing. I just watched him stumble into the room toward me.

"Reading a book? Ha! You boxers are so amusing," he slurred.

I looked up at him quietly.

His grin suddenly vanished and he muttered, "I'm not scared of you."

I looked at his bloated face; his cheeks were red pads of lawyer-fat. There are times when just because I keep my mouth shut and don't say what I think, I feel my strength growing. Still, I don't seem to know what I think till I actually say it. So I said nothing.

"Stand up!" he slurred.

I put the book down and stood. He walked up to me, put his face close to mine and blew cigar smoke into it. "I'm just as tough as you," he said.

"Yeah, right," I said under my breath.

"You think you could whip me?" he asked.

"No," I lied.

"Damn right, you couldn't." Then he raised his hand and slapped my face. My ears rang.

I swear, at that moment I looked at his lard face and I felt sorry for him.

"Reading a book. Ha! You'll *never* have my brains," he slurred. His jowls wobbled. "Did I ever tell you how many grades I skipped in school? Three. I skipped three grades. And I was *still* at the top of my class. At eighteen, I graduated with honors from Columbia University."

You're still stupid, I said to myself. You've read a thousand books, I bet, but you're still dead inside. I'll get more fun and fire out of my life than you'll ever get out of yours. I've got feelings, ideas and secrets inside me that you don't even know exist—because you're stupid. Maybe people'll laugh at me for saying someone running for state senator is a stupid bastard, especially when I can only mumble and stutter and add 8 + 5 and 7 + 6 on my fingers. But what I say is fact. You're stupid and I'm not because I'm alive inside and you're dead.

"What's wrong, son, cat got your tongue?" he asked.

"No," I said.

"You entered this boxing tournament illegally, didn't you?"

"Yeah."

"What would they do if they found that out?" He grinned.

"I don't know." You scumbag.

He sucked at his tooth. "They'd probably disqualify you, wouldn't they?"

"Maybe." He was stupid, yeah, but clever. I could see the lawyer-logic working—if there's a person, there's usually a jugular.

He grinned. "You *hate* me, don't you?"

"No. I don't hate you," I lied.

He raised his hand and slapped me again hard.

I didn't blink.

"You'd like to take a swing at me now, wouldn't you?"

"Not really," I lied.

"Go ahead." He waited.

I stared back at him quietly.

He raised his hand and back-slapped me. "Punch me back!" he shouted.

I didn't move.

"C'mon! Hit me!" He jutted out his jaw.

Just then his son Rodney traipsed into the room.

"Come here, Rodney!" ordered his father. "I want to show you something. Watch this!" He turned to me, and for the fifth time, smacked my face hard.

I saw stars, but I didn't give him the satisfaction of saying a damn thing.

Rodney's eyes bugged out.

"Ha! There's your tough boxer for you," slurred Ceffone as he stumbled out of the room, feeling like the prizefighter he never was.

The next morning while I was inside the murky darkness of my dream, the face smirked. The roller coaster—CLACKETY-CLACK—CLACKETY-CLACK—CLACKETY-CLACK— climbed. I slugged a left-right combination into the hole that was a mouth. POW! POW! Ceffone squealed joyfully like a pig.

I ripped into consciousness with a sneeze. My eyes snapped open, and I found yellow snot on my upper lip. My throat, scab-raw, ached—the fucking flu.

I blew my nose and studied the Rorschach test of yellow clotted mucus; it was the color of a yellow school bus.

I slumped into the musky stench of the white Sanforized
sheets. The fucking flu. Why me? After years of street fighting,
punching socks against walls, punching waves at low tide at the
Jersey shore pretending I was different heavyweight champions;
feinting at telephone poles, boxing moths at night on the porch,
slap-fighting in the school bathroom, shoveling snow and raking
leaves in an unnatural right-handed boxing stance, not blinking
my eyes when mowing lawns beneath branches, not blinking my
eyes with debris flying in car windshields—pretending it to be
punches . . .

I was a pussy.

A twenty-four-hour bug—big shit. Joe Gans, a former light-
weight champ, once had gone twenty-one rounds for the crown
while scuzzed up with tuberculosis. And Billy Miske, a heavyweight, once had fought for the title crippled with Bright's Disease.

Both got their asses kicked.

I looked up at the ceiling. Spiders, I noticed, had the moldings
under silent construction. In the corners, black bugs hung in
webs. Sucked dry. Everyone is on someone else's menu, I
thought. I hoped that *I* wasn't on my *own* menu.

I laid there in bed thinking. Joe Gans, Billy Miske, me. Then
I thought about Max Streets in a hospital bed curled up in a fetal
position. He was sucking his thumb—his big meaty thumb.
Wow.

Eating lunch, I could feel the germs congealing, coagulating
and colonizing in my throat.

Steak—each time I swallowed, I winced in pain.

Orange juice—each gulp, I winced in pain

TWELVE

THE SEMIFINALS

Making a Pearl

Broccoli—I winced in pain.

Pussy.

I was in the mood to beat myself up, so I swallowed saliva twenty-one times in succession (one gulp for every round Gans had fought). It made me feel better.

The kitchen clock said one.

Dust particles twirled and twisted in the sunlight. My mind became congested with Valerie. I thought about watching her eat, what she had called, "the harmony of vanilla ice cream and blueberry pie." It occurred to me that today alone she had probably laughed more than I had in the past three months. I squeezed out chuckles.

Why was I putting my miserable nervous system through this boxing crap while she was leading a normal life? I thought of her ironing her hair and painting her fingernails red and eating Twinkies.

And since entering this tournament, I've had liquid shits.

I hadn't fucked Valerie or pulled myself off for three very long

169

months. Two nights ago my cock had even gulped back a wet dream. Discipline!

And now my body gets sick. I fuck up everything in the end.

I bundled up warmly and jammed on my black porkpie hat. I drove to Temple Beth El to talk to God. The clouds, cerebrum gray, loomed angry and ominous.

While driving, I thought that I'd never have to do anything as shitty in my entire life as box: swallow a toad in the morning, and the rest of the day will be fine.

All I wanted was to be okay and to live a peaceful, normal life—and get rid of my fucking sore throat before my match tonight.

Tom locked the gym door and we walked down the street. He stopped in front of a brand new El Dorado and opened the door.

"Like it?" he asked, petting the candy-apple-red hood.

"Where'd you get this?" I laughed. I had expected to see his worm-eaten Impala.

He nodded knowingly. "You don't think I got friends?" He hopped in the driver's seat. His orange plaid shirt, which resembled Tex-co wallpaper, clashed violently with the red velvet interior.

I hopped in. Seeing an unshaven and brutally dressed guy like Tom sitting behind the wheel of a pimpmobile was comical.

"You don't think I got friends?" he repeated. "I got friends." He pumped the gas pedal and started the engine.

I sniffed back a gob of phlegm and swallowed.

"I got friends in high places and so could you," he said, "if you win tonight."

The car sped on. The rubber tires rolled smoothly over the flat asphalt toward the Holland Tunnel.

"Kemmelman asked me to give ya this," said Tom, flipping me a white envelope.

I opened it and read: "Good luck tonight, Pete. Kick ass. Win the whole thing. He who makes a beast of himself gets rid of the pain of being a man. Your Hebe friend—Bobby."

"What he say?"

"Wished me luck," I said, wondering.

"Nice guy, that Bobby—strange, but nice. "What is he now? Twenty-five?"

"I think so," I said, curious as to why Bobby had written such a note.

"You eighteen?"

"Yeah."

"I was thinking . . . ," said Tom.

"About?"

"You. I was wondering if you agree with me that it's about time you start planning."

"Planning what?"

"Your life."

"I guess," I said, listening to Jimi Hendrix's "If 6 Was 9" on the radio.

"Well, what do you want?" asked Tom.

"Want?"

"Outta life?"

"I'm not thinking that far. I'm thinking about tonight—now."

"Now! Now! A dog lives in the 'now,' " said Tom. "Listen, son—it's time you learn something about the facts of life." He snapped off the radio. "You're a talented boy. You got guts. You got brains. You got style. Where does it get you? Lemme tell ya—nowhere—not unless you plan."

I watched Tom tightly grip the steering wheel as if it might go somewhere.

"So tell me—what're your plans after the Gloves?"

I didn't know what to say.

"Hello? Hello? Is anybody home?" said Tom playfully. But he wasn't playing.

"I was thinking about college."

"College!" His mismatched eyes ignited. "You got curvature of the brain? Let me tell you about college. You got a little piece of sand in you that college ain't gonna touch."

"Sand?"

"You got a grain of sand wedged inside you, boy—just like a clam. And just like a clam you're gonna be makin' a pearl!"

"How's that?" I asked.

"By boxing! Look, as a kid I was in your shoes. I was angry, just like you. In other words—you got the germ inside you."

"Germ?"

"Look—say your body gets an infection, right? What does it do? Ignore it? No. Pretend it's not there? No. It fights. It builds antibodies. It makes pus. Snot. It doesn't go off to college to read books. You go to college and you're runnin'."

I didn't understand all of what he was saying; he was talking like a biology book.

"Listen to me," he said, soothingly, "I like you. The first time I seen you I says to myself—Now there's a kid who has the calling in him. Some guys have it to be priests but, son, you got the calling in you to be a fighter. Don't make the mistake I made and run away from it." Tom paused dramatically and looked deep into my eyes. "Wake up. The Lord's callin' you, boy."

I was flattered, but somehow Tom's mind reminded me of a Chinese infant's foot—bound and stunted. I had the feeling that maturity had set into Tom like rigor mortis.

"Sounds like you haven't buried the hatchet yet with your stepfather," I said.

"Hell, I buried the hatchet. I just remember where I buried it," he said, sounding like a middle-aged adolescent.

"Ha!" I laughed. What he said made some sense but somehow, I felt, his reasoning was unsound. It was like getting mad at a mud puddle and then kicking it. I suspected that Tom's life was one big grunt, and that the lessons he'd learned had amounted not to wisdom, but to scar tissue and callus.

"Go pro!" he said with vengence—a vengeance that I saw would last his lifetime.

"I'll think about it," I said. I looked at him through the corner of my eye and in a vague way I wondered if boxing wasn't a remedy worse than the disease.

*　*　*

We drove out the Holland Tunnel and hit a smell that **was** New York City: wharf garbage, the shit-drab Hudson and exhaust fumes. New York City smelled like the dead air inside a basketball.

My throat was killing me, but I didn't want to tell Tom. What good would it do?

We drove north on Tenth past brick warehouses and abandoned buildings.

"Look at that," said Tom, pointing.

I looked, hoping it was a whore. I liked looking at whores. I'm always curious as to why they do it. Instead, it was only a dog with a bone in its mouth. It stood in the middle of Twenty-fifth Street scratching at a pothole.

"Probably the only dirt it can find is in that pothole," I said.

"You gotta give that mutt credit—he's ballsy enough to risk his mangy little life to dig in the middle of a city street."

"He is what he is," I said, thinking.

Tom suddenly found a parking spot.

"Lock up," he said. "I don't want nobody breakin' in."

"So this *is* your car," I said.

"Mine?" Tom peered at me and laughed. "It's *yours!*"

"Mine?" I gasped, holding in nerve-piss.

"If you sign with us and go pro," he said, jiggling the keys in the palm of his hand.

I looked at the candy-apple-red car. It *was* beautiful. Valerie would love it.

"Sleep on it," said Tom, thumping me on the back.

Just then, the same mutt pattered past, its head hung low, its fur matted and filthy.

"I like puppies," observed Tom. "Too bad they gotta grow up to be dogs."

As we walked to the Garden, I noticed a hardware store. Its large neon sign read: A O K #1 HARDWARE. It's a secret message, I thought. I knew "HARDWARE" really meant "hard wear." Then I reversed the sign to read: HARD WEAR # 1 K

O A. I'm getting kayoed in the first round tonight—that's the message. But who's "A"?

Jones's first name was *A*men.

In the dressing room, I stepped into my jock and slipped on my green nylon trunks.

"Get ready for your draw," said Tom, picking his teeth with his forefinger.

I laced my shoes and waited for the official to call the subnovice middleweights. Like an empty egg, there was a fundamental brainlessness about me. I yawned and burped.

However, I began wondering about Kemmelman. He thought too much. If he were me now, his mind would be churning, "Who am I fighting tonight?" Should I shove my opponent in order to psyche him out? What would I do if my opponent said "Fuck you!" to me? If one of the semifinalists doesn't show, will I get a bye? Should I tell Tom about my sore throat so I'll have an excuse if I lose? . . .

"SUBNOVICE MIDDLEWEIGHTS!"

My mind slammed shut, and I stopped being Bobby Kemmelman and resumed being me—nothing.

"Griffith?" called out a froggy-voiced official.

"Here," said a pug voice.

"Valero?"

"Here."

"Jones, or is it Jonas?"

"Don't matter," spat Jones, "still's a slave name."

The white official ignored the comment.

"Watt?"

I nodded my head.

"I'll explain the procedure, boys," said the official. "Each fighter pulls a number outta the hat. Number one fights number two. Number three fights number four. Got it?"

Silence.

"Okay, pick."

In school, I had learned the one reason it is so easy to march men off to war is that each soldier feels deeply sorry for the man marching next to him who will die. Each protects himself in this fantasy until he's shocked to find out that it is he who is bleeding. With fighters it's similar—when they're lying bloody on the canvas.

Jones, Griffith, Valero and I took turns picking from the hat.

"Three," said Valero.

"Four," muttered Griffith, tossing his paper onto the desk.

"One," I said. I glanced at Jones. He stood six-three, but his afro made him look six-eight.

"Good luck," he said, not offering his hand, "you'll need it."

Refusing to be buried, the secret message came back to me: HARD WEAR #1 K O A.

In the ring, Jones wore army-camouflage trunks. Eyes popping, he gnawed at his mouthpiece and sneered. He looked like a madman frothing at the mouth. In fact, he was frothing. Maybe he was angry because I had knocked out Green, his stable partner. Or maybe he was upset because I looked like someone he didn't like—a white person.

CLANG!

Jones rushed and whipped out a triple jab—each one a bull's-eye on my nose. His reach was so long that I couldn't believe I was being hit. I was because I felt the blood. I crouched, but five authoritative splats bounced onto my head. I covered myself with forearms and gloves. He snaked in a right hand. I took it solidly on the eye and saw a black-blue-red-green colored color. Another jab speared me. He was beating my ass. Suddenly, I could feel the crowd watching me. I looked like a sissy. I backpedaled into the ropes. Jones chased. From a distance, he jammed a hard right into my face that bent my nose about 180 degrees. Lie down, pansy, I told myself, tasting blood. Lie down!

Desperately, I clinched. You're sick! I whispered. You shouldn't be fighting. Hell, you shouldn't even be a fighter in the first place! With the next punch tumble over! Pretend to get knocked out!

White trash.

"BREAK!" barked the ref.

We both stepped back.

"BOX!"

I stepped low, planted my foot, and with a grunt I came up with a slashing left hook that was the best fucking punch in the history of my miserable life. It landed with a mushy thud. One second Jones was there, the next, he wasn't. He was lying at my feet in an unconscious, sweaty pile. The shot was a solid piece of hope; it was a tire-iron knocking his jaw into his throat. It was a collision that I'd often dreamt about and Jones had probably had nightmares over.

The crowd shrieked five octaves higher. They kept yelling as the doctor, the ref and handlers huddled around Jones.

"STEP BACK!" yelled the doctor.

I stood staring at Jones's fluttering eyelids and twitching feet. Have you ever seen a dog take a crap and then, after he's finished, sniff it? That's what I felt like as I looked at Jones—a dog sniffing and inspecting his own shit.

The ref raised my arm and the announcer bellowed, "THE WINNER BY KNOCKOUT IN FORTY-NINE SECONDS OF THE FIRST ROUND—IRISH PETE WATT!!!" With tears in his eyes, Tom raced to center ring and lifted me off my feet. Then he set me down and pulled my mouthguard from my mouth.

"I'm sick," I said, my throat on fire.

"I KNOW! I KNOW!" he said, misunderstanding, but hugging me lovingly.

I had never seen a guy look so happy while he was crying.

"Okay, Watt," said an official in the weighing room. "We need a snapshot of you and some personal info for the readers so they know who you are."

"Okay."

The photographer stood before me. I emptied my face of everything.

SNAP!

"Hudson High, right?" asked the official, looking at a card.

"Yeah," I lied, studying his reaction.

"Do you participate in any extracurricular activities at Hudson High?"

"Football and baseball."

"Any academic honors or awards?"

"No."

"Do you have a job?"

"No."

"Any hobbies?"

"No."

"Music? Dancing?"

"No."

"Do you play any instruments?"

"No."

"This isn't gonna be much of a bio, is it, kid?"

I shrugged.

"Do you want to add anything else?"

"No."

"Do you wanna make any statements?"

"No."

"Okay, that's it, then," he said, shrugging.

I walked back to the dressing room. I'll be damned if I was going to tell anybody about me playing saxophone or being in the school band or collecting stamps.

Tom talked while I put on my socks. I wasn't listening, but I heard him anyway.

". . . the cells in your brain have all these fanfuckingtastic images that stretch back to the Stone Age. I want those cells to grow . . ."

"And multiply?" I asked.

"You got it now!" sung out Tom.

"Huh?" I had finally realized that Tom was a species unto himself.

"Son, when you hit people with that left hook, they go down. It's like a law of nature!"

I grimaced.

"You know the thing I said before, about 'the calling'? I've only met one other fella who had it."

"Yeah, who?"

"Well, it don't matter who—I lost him—or I should say, he lost himself. Poor guy, he went off to college." Tom glanced at me, his good eye glistening like a galvanized marble. "Now some people say college is good—and it might be—but I still say it's better to heed God's call and be a fighter. By the way, I heard from some reliable people that after college the guy turned out to be queer-bait." Tom shook his head mournfully.

"Tom, I don't feel so good," I said, rubbing my throat.

"Don't worry, I'll fix ya up," he winked. "We'll take it easy in the gym for a few days."

"Who'll I spar, Kemmelman?"

He shook his head. "Funny guy, Kemmelman. He told me that he ain't comin' back no more."

"He quit?"

"I guess."

"He who makes a beast of himself gets rid of the pain of being a man."

"What?"

"Nothing."

As we walked out of the dressing room, Tom asked, "How's your throat?"

"Hurts."

"Ever eat Vaseline?"

"Eat Vaseline?"

"It's an old trick," he boasted. "You stick with me, son, and we'll make that pearl!"

We walked east toward the pimpmobile.

"Did I ever tell you about how I taught myself to be a cut man?"

"No."

"Well, every pro needs a good cut man, and people know I'm the best in the business, see? I got newspaper clippings to prove it!"

"Yeah?"

"I never told this before, but I practice on cats."

"Cats?"

"Strays. First I shave 'em, then I cut 'em up and then I practice with different types of concoctions to patch 'em up again."

"No," I said, not believing—not wanting to believe.

"Oh, yeah! It really works—no scars or nothing'." His one eye glistened. "Let's take care of that throat of yours," he said, looking in his duffle bag. "I think I have some Vaseline in here somewheres."

THIRTEEN

THE GYM

A Plan

The smell of roast beef hung in the air.

"I never thought," said my stepfather, rowing a spoon through his coffee, "that you'd make it this far."

"But you did it, sweetie," chirped my mother, "you made it to the finals."

She inhabited my soul, my mother, yet she was at the same time a stranger. How could she stay married to a guy who tried to stab her? Money, I guessed, and maybe habit.

The rest of my family hunched forward slurping away at roast beef, potatoes and chopped carrots.

"Do you want some more mashed potatoes, Peter?" offered the maid.

"No," I wheezed, my lungs bags of snot. The mashed potatoes were soft and good; it was about the only thing that I could swallow—other than Vaseline. But I hadn't trained in five days, and I was concerned about gaining weight.

"What did Dr. Nagle tell you today, honey?" asked my mother, chewing carrots.

"Liquids 'n' rest," my voice phlegmed.

Lance looked at me. "I have the perfect cure for your sore throat—cut it. Pass the meat, please."

"Is he giving you antibiotics?" asked my mother, ignoring Lance.

"Yeah, shots and pills," I croaked, coughing in a series of racking spasms. I took a napkin from my lap, hawked and spat yellowish-brown phlegm into it that looked a lot like butterscotch pudding.

"Oh, dear!" exclaimed my mother.

I had inherited my father's lungs, but I have to be thankful. If he had had good lungs, he would have sailed to France in 1943 and have been slaughtered on the beach like the rest of his troop, and my brother and I would never have been born.

"I'll be fine," I rasped, knowing my fight was only four days away.

"Of course you will," snapped Ceffone, bruising the air with his voice. "You've come this far, you can't quit. In fact, a number of gentlemen and I at the club are placing bets on you to beat Valero. Valero's not much of a fighter. He was darn lucky to knock out Griffith."

"Americo Valero uncorked a devastating right hand to the shaven head of Abe Griffith to score a knockout in 2:05 of the first round," is how the New York *Daily News* had put it.

Something wiggled in the cocoon of my mind. "May I please be excused?" I asked.

"Are you all right, sweetie?" asked my mother.

"Yeah, I just want to lie down."

"Certainly, dear."

"Pass the milk, please," said Rodney blankly.

When I'm sick in bed wearing thermal underwear, I get a lot of time to think. And when I'm through thinking about the stuff I want to think about, I begin to think about the stuff I don't want to think about—like people betting on me. Guys at school were probably wagering, too. That week I'd probably blown a pound of snot out my nostrils. Didn't people understand I was sick? Did they need evidence?

A particle of thought flickered in my mind; it was a little scratching in the corner of my brain—an irritating something. It grew to be the size of a fist, and it drove squarely into the middle of my consciousness. It was . . . a plan.

Three days later I walked into Brandy's Gym feeling okay. It was the day before my fight and that morning I had eaten what I believed to be the last Vaseline of my life; (it does bad things on the other end). Normally, I should have been resting but I hadn't trained in ten days.

"Fine fucking time to get the flu," squawked Tom, seeing me. "How you feel now?"

"Okay."

"What say you go three rounds and we see what you got?"

"Sure," I said. I had my plan set.

"Get the gloves."

As I flipped the dial on my lock I thought about the soft-hitting Bobby Kemmelman. He would have fit into my plan good. "Too bad Kemmelman ain't around no more. I'd like to spar him," I murmured.

Tom whitened. "What! You didn't hear?"

"What?"

"Kemmelman's dead."

"Dead?"

"He killed himself."

"What?"

"He committed suicide. Cops found him lying in the front seat of his car in his garage—carbon monoxide poisoning."

"No!" I couldn't believe it.

"His wife was found dead, too."

"Why'd he do it?"

"Who knows?" shrugged Tom.

I walked to Bobby's locker and opened it. It was cleared out. Penciled to the inside of the locker was the message: HE WHO

MAKES A BEAST OF HIMSELF GETS RID OF THE PAIN OF BEING
A MAN.

The only other thing left was a faint skin of dust.

I got dressed and walked onto the gym floor prepared to spar
Sullivan, the scumbag. I wrapped my hands as I watched Miguel
Barahona spar with a young kid.

Miguel moved about the ring, as usual, on his heels. Each
punch, thud, thud, knocked his head, thud, thud, back sharply,
scarring his, thud, thud, brain. Miguel still came to the gym to
fight even though he had been retired for years. I knew that he
was a bachelor who worked the graveyard shift as a night watch-
man. It occurred to me that being punched was possibly the only
human contact Miguel ever got—maybe he even needed it.

In the far corner, plastering a heavy bag, was Wepner. He was
at the end of his workout, and his sweaty face looked so soft, pink
and moist that, I swear, it could have been spread with a pliable
butter knife.

I thought of Kemmelman.

I love fighters. I admit it. I wanted to be one myself. They are
the gutsyest people in the whole world. But if Tom was right
about me, that I had "a calling" to be a fighter, then God was
a dangerous maniac who should be shot.

Four older gentlemen, businessmen types, stood in the gym
doorway. I noticed them immediately because they kept pretending not to be staring at me. No one had to tell me who they
were—they were the El Dorado people.

Blood pounded in my ears, and my lips were parched dry. I
swiveled my neck from side to side. I had my plan.

"Stick your hand in," said Tom, offering me a warm glove, wet
and heavy from Barahona. He flashed me a vicious look—"Fight
good!" said his face. "You'd better fight good. I don't want
excuses, no mess-ups, no nothin'. I spent a lot of time trainin'
you—don't screw up now."

The bell rang, and Sullivan and I touched gloves—a gym rule.

To carry out my plan with a slime like Sullivan hurt, but I had to choose—go through with it or not. I felt a tug of war within me. Inside, a voice kept saying, "No, no. This is wrong!" Another voice said, "Yes, yes! It won't hurt anything." Choosing was tough—it was painting myself into a corner.

"Pick your spots! Pick your spots!" hollered Tom from the ring apron.

Sullivan danced away cautiously—he knew my sparring style had no happy medium. He darted out two jabs that landed. Jabs don't normally hurt, but these stung; I figured it was my cold. I chased him and threw a left hook that missed.

"Upstairs—Downstairs! In and out!" yelled Tom.

The businessmen watched. The trolls watched.

Sullivan again threw two jabs. I brushed them away, muscled him to the ropes, banged a few body shots and shuffled back. I waited for him to muster enough courage to throw his right hand—I knew I could time it properly.

Suddenly, he threw it—the right. I stuck out my chin, rolled with the punch and fell flat on the floor.

I lay on the canvas, knocked out; but really I was standing up explaining to everybody I was sick. I was showing what I could never say outright; despair is not something I share with others. I lay on the canvas, knocked out; but really I was fabricating an excuse to alleviate the pressure. I lay on the canvas, knocked out; but really I was standing in front of a mirror. "You are learning," said the mirror, "that either the world is too strong for you or you're too weak for it."

Sure, I finally got up and finished my bullshit skit by ranting and raving like an idiot. Tom and two fighters fell for it and jumped into the ring to restrain me.

But the damage was done; I was introduced to myself. I broke, I snapped—I had found my weak link. And knowing that hurt.

As I walked into the dressing room I felt a great sense of relief mix with a great sense of shame. I wished I could take it all back because if there was anything I wished not to find the day before the finals, it was further evidence of my lack of self-worth.

* * *

I was alone toweling off in the dressing room when a troll strolled in. It was the talky Latino with the badly broken nose. I had thought it would be Tom, but I figured he was outside explaining things to the El Dorado people.

"*Muchacho,* how you feel?" said the troll with concern.

"Okay," I said.

"Why you haven't been coming to the gym?" he asked, hunched within his gray overcoat.

"Sick."

"*Enfermo?*"

"*Si,*" I said, knowing a few words from Spanish class.

"You been training?" he asked.

"Couldn't." I quickly thought about what Tom had once told me—a boxer has only his body—no bat, no racket, no piano, only his fists. Physical condition, a fighter's essence, is attached to his training like his arm is to his shoulder.

"Too bad," said the broken-faced troll. "Still, you be fine tomorrow night—you *muy fuerte.*"

"Thanks," I said.

He watched me dress. Trolls weren't allowed in the dressing room, but I didn't mind, it wasn't my rule.

"*Usted como un toro,*" he quipped, clubbing his chest.

I looked at his smiling face. Nice guy, I thought.

"I be there tomorrow night. I watch you fight. You go three rounds?"

"Can I go three rounds?" I asked.

"*Si.* You got . . . how you say . . . energy?"

"I think," I said, hoping.

"*Bueno suerte, muchacho!*" said the troll, patting my back. Then he began laughing.

Yeah, I got energy, I told myself as the troll shuffled out the door. But I wondered.

I wondered as I drove home and I wondered as I lay in bed and I kept on wondering . . .

FOURTEEN

THE FINALS

. . . until I found myself in the Madison Square Garden dressing room on fight night.

"We's made it, buddy," grinned Mudbone Hopkins.

"Yeah," I sighed, leaning my head lazily onto the concrete wall.

The finals were juicy status, and a Golden Gloves title was serious—second only to the president of the United States of America.

But I was too relaxed. It was as if I'd reached my final destination and I could sit down. Was my goal, all along, just to reach the finals? Or was it to win the title? I just didn't feel that grain of sand Tom had talked about.

"Is irritation stimulation or is stimulation irritation?" Mrs. Simon once had asked us in English class.

I opened my eyes as an official called out, "MORALES! YOU'RE ON!"

I watched Candido Morales swivel his little Puerto Rican neck and scamper lemminglike out of the room. Let's face it—body shattering *is* the point of boxing just like killing is of war.

Big shit.

"I don't want you guys gettin' Gardenitis out there tonight," warned Tom, taping up Mudbone's shoelaces.

I burped.

"Remember, this ain't no different than any other fight."

"Only twenty-four thousand more people watchin', dat's all!" quipped Mudbone.

"Deal with it!" said Tom.

"Today, at work, I saw a bumper sticker," said Mudbone. " 'A WOMAN WITHOUT A MAN IS LIKE A FISH WITHOUT A BICY-CLE.' "

Tom scrunched up his face. "What does that mean?"

"I don't know," said Mudbone. "I thought maybe you'd know." Mudbone shrugged. "I just read it."

"I didn't know you black guys could read," said Tom.

My mind was buried in a black hole torquing toward Valero. Ceffone *lectured:* "Work Valero's belly—we got money riding on you." Steve Turner *suggested:* "During a clinch, bite the Spic's shoulder—thumb his eye." Tommy Crooks *recommended:* "Watch out for Valero's right hand after his jab." My father *urged:* "Be careful and keep your chin in." Valerie *cautioned:* "Protect your cock." The gray book *instructed:* "HOW TO BOX A JABBER—1) Keep low 2) Slip to the inside or outside guard position 3) Counter to the body 4) Try to time a right cross 5) Force continually." Coach Sgro *advised:* "Move close and cold-cock him with your left." Mr. Goldsmith *counseled:* "Think positive. Believe you can beat Valero and you will." My brother Dan *wrote* (in a letter from his drug rehabilitation center): "Dear Champ! I read in the *Daily News* that Valero wants to bust up my baby brother's intestines. Don't let him! I'm counting on you to be strong. All the guys in here are rooting for you (even the

PR's!). I'm sorry I can't be there to cheer you on! Love, Dan."
I yawned.

For three months I had pumped up in order to reach the finals.
And now the pump eased down into a relaxation, almost a
mental and physical fatigue. I had never before in my life worked
as hard for anything. Training had sucked from me every breath,
every thought and every inch of energy, and now I felt limp.

I sat with my eyes shut just wishing to be taken as a stream
does a trout, smooth and easy the rest of the way.

Stimulation *was* irritation.

Maybe it was my weight. At the morning weigh-in, I scaled
one hundred and fifty-seven; six pounds less than normal. Tom
had a shit-fit. He rushed me to Gallagher's Steakhouse and had
me drink a glass of beef blood.

"GARCIA! YOU'RE ON!" called the official.

Sugar Garcia, wearing a sombrero, excited, feinting punches.

"You nervous?" asked Mudbone.

I shook my head and spit.

"It's true," said Mudbone, "what dey say about you, ain't it?"

I glanced at him and wondered. What had he heard?

"Too bad about Kemmelman, huh?" he said, changing the
subject.

I nodded.

"He was good people—why you think he did it?"

"Hopkins," said Tom, "worry about yourself, not Kemmelman."

"Tom," said Mudbone, "I can worry about myself till my
armpits run outta water, but there ain't no sense worryin' 'bout
things you got control over 'cause if you got control over 'em,
ain't no sense worryin'. And there ain't no sense worryin' about
the things you got no control over 'cause if you got no control
over 'em, ain't no sense worryin'!"

"Thin philosophy, ain't it, Pete?" asked Tom.

I tried to think of a reply, but couldn't. Maybe that's why I fought—because I couldn't think. My mouth was merely a grave for my tongue.

"I'll kayo Stewart in one round, and if I don't kayo him in one round, I'll kayo him in another!" exclaimed Mudbone.

I listened to something squish in Mudbone's stomach.

"Pepsi," he said, smirking.

"ANTUOFERMO! YOU'RE ON!" called the official.

Antuofermo, a muscular welterweight, knelt down, crossed himself and exited.

Very few fighters, I noticed, were atheists.

I looked at the other boxers scattered in the room. A heavy-weight slept, burbling little snores; three kids were curled up in depressions; and one dude, with cotton in his ears, read *The Exorcist.*

"Pete," said Mudbone, "let me teach ya some advice. It's a technique I use. It makes steppin' into da ring easy."

"What's that?"

"When you's climbin' through da ropes and standin' in the middle of da ring and all those fuckin' people is watchin' ya," said Mudbone, "just pretend, man, it ain't you."

He was serious. By my sixth fight, I could recognize emotion in a voice or an eye.

"Hopkins," scoffed Tom, "you need a checkup from the neck up."

"What you mean?" whined Mudbone indignantly.

"A shrink," barked Tom.

"PHELPS? YOU'RE NEXT!" called an official.

Phelps, the blackest kid I've ever seen in my life, exited yawn-ing.

Tom yawned.

I yawned. Tears watered my eyes.

"Cryin'?" asked Mudbone.

"Ain't cryin'," I snapped.

Mudbone nodded his head. "It *is* true what the guys in the gym say about ya."

"Hopkins," said Tom, "shut up and read something." He threw Mudbone the fight program.

Mudbone flipped it open. Inside were photos of the finalists. "Look at dese minimum-wage boys—look like dey be from inside a garbage can."

I slid closer.

He was referring to the thirty-six toughest mothers in New York City. And my picture was right there with them.

"There's your guy," I said, pointing to a kid who looked capable of ignoring great pain.

"Meat in the morgue," scoffed Mudbone.

"There's yours," said Mudbone pointing. Americo Valero had lopsided nostrils, a cauliflower ear and a geodesic afro.

"Guy's a slow-thinkin' slum dweller if I ever saw one," quipped Mudbone.

"A slow-thinkin' slum dweller who'll quickly beat the piss outta ya, if ya don't watch out," added Tom, munching at his middle knuckle.

Mudbone continued browsing the page. "Tell me this clown don't do drugs."

It was a picture of a long-haired, 112-pounder with a shit-eating grin. He reminded me of my hippie brother Dan.

"My brother," I said softly, "does drugs."

"No," said Mudbone, surprised.

"Smack."

"He a junkie?"

"Since he was sixteen," I said.

"He still shootin'?"

I shook my head. "He stopped, I think. At least . . . I hope."

"I hope so, too, buddy," said Mudbone, patting my thigh.

You're okay, Mudbone, I thought.

To pass time, I inspected the other photos on the page. They looked like mug shots from a medieval bestiary. Earl Broadnax, a black stud with bushy muttonchops, scowled; Shobe Stumbo, a bald-headed freak with a cross tattooed to his cheek, deadpanned; a gap-toothed Leroy Collazo looked as if he belonged in a wooden crate destined for the Bronx Zoo; smirking Rugy Daniels, beetle-browed and thick-necked, appeared to be a very, very disturbed individual; slack-jawed Tyrone Tripp, not a very handsome guy, looked to be endowed with the same I.Q. as that of a sea sponge; Nathan Capo resembled a high-quality degenerate—his teeth stuck out like pegs and his head resembled a lava rock covered with skin. Then there was Pete Watt. He may have looked tough, but inside he was wall-to-wall carpeting and big, soft pillows.

That's why I was so proud to be sitting with those guys. In a way, they were the strong ones—even sane ones.

I watched Shobe Stumbo, a heavyweight, fumble with the knob of his portable radio . . . The Temptations. If I had my choice, I'd do some Kinks or Animals, or even better, one of my father's beautiful songs.

Silently, I sang "The Little Boy."

After squeezing out a leak in the bathroom, I peeked out into the corridor. Walking down the hall was the broken-nosed troll.

"Hey!" I called. "What you doing here?"

"Watt!" he exclaimed.

"Why are you back here?"

"I told you I'd come, didn't I?" he said.

"I figured you'd be in the audience."

"Yeah, well, *chico* . . . I got a fighter in the finals."

I looked at the round trainer sticker attached to his sweater. "No fooling! Who?"

"My son," he said.

"I didn't know you had a son who boxed."

The troll grinned.

"Well, tell him to kick ass!"

"He will," smiled the troll. He turned to leave, then looked back. "How's your cold tonight?"

"Okay."

"Buena suerte."

* * *

"Mudbone. Guess who I was just talking with in the hallway," I said.

"I don't know, but guess who Tom is talking with in the bathroom."

"Who?"

"Officials."

"So?"

"Man, dey found out you ain't Jersey City. They ain't lettin' you fight."

My heart bounced.

Tom walked in. On each side of him stood a top Golden Gloves official. Both wore pinstripe suits.

"You're not from Jersey City are you, son?" demanded one of the pinstripes.

I looked at Tom, who coughed nervously.

"You snuck into our tournament illegally, didn't you?"

Quietly, I burped and tasted beef blood.

"We know that you live in Rockleigh. And we know that you attend Old Tappan High School."

Something sharp pinched and squeezed my stomach.

"Isn't that correct?"

I nodded my head.

"Since you falsified information, we could prevent you from fighting—are you aware of that?"

Again I nodded.

"You broke the rules, son."

They both stared down at me.

I said softly, "Let me fight . . . please."

They stared silently.

"Please, my friends . . ."

"What about your friends?" asked a pinstripe.

"They all came. They're all here to see me fight . . . I don't want to let them down." My blood pounded.

"You *did* sell quite a few tickets," said a pinstripe, cracking a smile. "Probably a record—wouldn't you say, Simon?"

"Perhaps," said Simon.

"Please, sir," I begged, "let me fight."

The officials looked at me. One said, "We spoke with your coach already and have decided to let you fight on only one condition."

My eyes widened.

"Give the crowd a good show and kick ass."

"Thank you, thank you," I whispered to them. And screw you, Ceffone, I thought to myself.

"WATT! YOU'RE ON!" called an official.

"We're on!" said Tom, hopping up nervously.

"I'm on, I'm on," I repeated, eyes wide.

"Be cool!" advised Mudbone. "Just pretend you ain't there."

I nodded.

"Who's your favorite team?" asked Mudbone.

"Me! I'm my favorite team," I said, smiling.

"Dat's cool, breeze!"

"Let's go," said Tom.

On the other side of the ring was Americo Valero. Standing at his side, kneading his neck, was the broken-nosed troll!

"That fuckin' Spic!" growled Tom above the crowd's roar. "That cocksuckin' . . ." The arena swallowed the rest.

Nothing prepares an eighteen-year-old kid for Madison Square Garden—the hot lights, the crowd, the pressure, the TV coverage. I flailed my arms apelike and prayed.

During instructions, Valero grinned. He knew I'd been sick; he knew about my left hook; he knew I'd been "floored" sparring; shit, he probably knew I used to wet the bed.

I walked back to the corner and said, "Tom, I hope . . ."

"You will! You will!" he said, jamming in my mouthpiece. "Just rush Across and beat his ass!"

The bell rang.

Valero came out dancing. His long jab licked the air about my face. They were fear jabs. I slipped inside and tried to bang the belly but he tied me up easily. Close to his mouth, I smelled French fries.

The ref broke us.

Valero continued to jab and move to my right. He knew my hook would break his skull if it landed.

Each of his jabs was missing by fractions. To dodge them, I swiveled my neck—no ducking, parrying or sidestepping—I had to conserve energy.

Half-heartedly, I pressed him onto the ropes. Trapped, he threw a wild right—but it wasn't too wild because it nailed my nose. He flurried and I held on. His arms were slick with Vaseline. Toward the end of the round, I realized I was giving him the round—I wasn't doing shit, except conserving energy. He was at least doing something—punching.

The bell rang.

"Get with it!" yelled Tom.

"Tired."

"I don't care! Fight!" he shouted, slapping my face.

I sucked in air, blew it out, sucked in air, blew it out.

The bell rang.

Valero got ballsier. He started stepping in with his jabs and began scoring. I cranked out my hook but he skipped and sidestepped away gracefully. I saw something white on his lips. I thought it was his mouthpiece but it was foam; he was definitely up.

I rushed at him but his skilled footwork enabled him to change directions. It was like arguing with my stepfather—he, too, had a way of changing tacks so you could never pin him down.

Down in the seats, there was a lot of screaming. My friends waved large bedsheet banners reading:

> WATT! THE ROCKLEIGH CLOUTER!
> GOOD LUCK WATT!
> WE LOVE IRISH PETE WATT

Maybe that's why I fought—to win back friends. It was good to hear their cheers.

But I was losing the fight. Valero stepped in and one-twoed me; I saw black and clinched. I felt blood ooze from my nose. I tried to prod my mind into rage but couldn't. It just wasn't there.

The bell rang. I walked to my corner.

Tom didn't have the stool ready. He was still on the floor fussing with bottles and towels. To rest, stupid me decided to squat onto the lower ring rope. It gave way and I tumbled onto the canvas.

"OOOHHH!!" cried the crowd.

"We're losin' it!" Tom said, sitting me down. "We gotta knock him out, hear? Go to him . . . let your hook fly . . . breathe!" He wiped the blood from my face. "Knock him out, okay? OKAY?"

He was pleading. But I felt hollow. This was the third round coming up, and I had to do it. "Okay," I gasped.

The bell rang.

I rushed from my corner and bored into Valero's chest without grace, without skill, not even worried anymore. Valero tried to run, but I trapped him in the corner and slammed his face and body with lefts and rights. Accidentally on purpose, I let one or two hooks stray below his belt. The crowd was exploding.

The ref broke us, checked Valero's eyes for glass, and motioned us to continue.

I joe-fraziered forward. Bobbing and weaving, I came up with a left hook that spluttered onto his chin. He sagged. Gasping, I splattered his face like I did the rolled-up socks in the basement. Valero's body rolled like liquid.

The bell rang! The crowd went wild.

Tom hugged and kissed me in the corner. "I'm proud of ya, son," he said.

"D' I win?" I gasped.

Tom smiled nervously and said, "We'll see."

I walked to center ring. The ref grabbed my wrist, and Valero, me and the ref waited for the decision. I knew it was close. I shut my eyes and hoped, prayed, that they'd give me the edge because I was white.

The announcer tapped the mike. Silence blanketed the crowd. "THE WINNER OF THE 1971 SUBNOVICE MIDDLE-WEIGHT CLASS IS VALERO! VALERO!"

I'd blown it. I was the big favorite and I choked. Shame saturated me. I wanted to crawl into the nearest rat hole and hide.

Back in the dressing room, I held my head and thought of how I had let down my friends.

"Suckers robbed us!" wailed Tom.

I could tell that Tom wanted to explode royally but he couldn't because he still had to work with Mudbone.

"Just 'cause we're from Jersey they rob us!" he fumed. He kicked at a burnt-out butt on the floor. "Bastards!"

"HOPKINS! YOU'RE ON!" called an official.

Tom stamped out of the room; Mudbone pranced behind.

Alone, reflecting, I toed the dead butt. "Fuck me," I thought. "I suck. I always screw up things in the end. I let down my friends. I'm a loser. I'm a Max Streets." After ten minutes of self-pity and feeling like a huge Caucasian failure, I decided to shower.

As I stepped into the stall and got the water going, I began to think about my life and the person I'd become—a Golden Gloves fighter. I began to cry—I mean *cry.*

I've heard of fighters going crazy after losing—like George Foreman, the heavyweight champion. Jesus Christ actually visited George while he was lying on the rubbing table. Jake Lamotta saw God. Me? I began to go, I guess, a bit hysterical.

"Hey! You okay in there?" yelled a voice.

I wailed.

"Stop bangin' your head on the wall!" yelled the nervous voice.

My brain was a bag of crazy thoughts and ideas. I realized that boxing had been a minor form of suicide. During ten years' fighting, my mind had become a corpse. Why waste energy thinking? I twisted Peter Watt into an unthinking animal armed with instinct. Boxing reinforced a dullness in my mind so I wouldn't ooze in anxiety and fear.

It was an alienation of myself, something like burying a mirror. Holy shit, it took thousands of rounds of sparring to say that sentence.

I wept.

As I stood there bawling like a three-year-old I thought suddenly of the good things boxing had given me. It provided the task, and taste, of growing up. It was my *irrational* rational decision to build a firm and strong foundation from which to start my life. Most important, fighting was a challenge. It helped me prove that "soft" guys like my father and me, and people like us, could do "hard" things and excel at them—even surpass those bastards like my stepfather. It gave me permission to be myself.

I began to calm down. I stopped pounding my head against the shower stall. The whole thing came to me in the form of a simple and powerful feeling, like one of my father's songs. I stood there with the water pouring down and tried to feel the texture of my feelings and understand what it meant. I realized that I didn't need to fight anymore. I had rid myself of it. There were other challenges now—a new world.

My fists unclenched. Fighting was behind me.

But there was a twinge of sadness. The past three months in the Golden Gloves was a priceless morsel of life. What would I do next? What would take its place? Without boxing I no longer was going to have that mental and physical confrontation anymore, and what worried me was that the prospect made me feel good.

After I dressed and combed my hair, I walked into the officials' room to pick up the *one thing* that proved that I was not just an ordinary kid; the *one thing* that proved that I was exceptional; the *one thing* that proved that it was all worthwhile—the Golden Gloves necklace.

"Here ya go, Watt. Congratulations!" said an official. He handed me a silver necklace with a boxing glove pendant studded with a ruby. The winners got the same necklace, only it was gold, studded with a diamond.

I looked at it; it was beautiful. It was status. Without it, I would be just another kid in the crowd. I clutched it pitifully. "Thank you," I said.

"Looks good!" commented the official.

I looked at myself in the mirror and soared with delight. For once, I recognized myself for what I was—different. I was my own person, not anyone else—*me*.

I knew that it was a little disgusting to need a necklace to make me feel good.

"Be back next year, Watt?" asked the official.

"I don't know. Maybe," I said.

"Well, good luck to you—you're one helluva fighter, kid!"

"Thank you."

I walked out the door and down the hallway. Boxing, like my love for tin soldiers, I realized, could not survive the test of time. I'd never loved fighting—but I'd *worshiped* it. I had thrown myself into fighting with a passion—it was fire and magic. I had paid a high price for living with that single dream of reaching the Golden Gloves. It had shaped my life and defined me. It had been the dark eyeglasses that I did not see when I looked through them. And now it was finished. I was tired of my obsession.

"Watt!" called someone from behind.

I turned and saw the troll.

"Watt," he said, approaching, "I know you mad, but I explain, *por favor.*"

I glanced at the diamond-studded necklace held in his hand.

"Americo is my son. I feared for him. He is not a born fighter, like you. He get beat up in the gym each day by Green and Jones, you beat both Green and Jones, I must do something. I go to your gym and watch you train. I help *mi hijo,* see?"

"Americo fought a good fight."

"He won," said the troll, "because you was sick."

I shrugged. "He won because he fought good," I repeated, not wanting to diminish their victory.

"I trained him to stay away from your left hand," said the troll.

"He won fair and square."

"Yes," said the troll, nodding his head. "But you are the *tiger.*"

"No problem," I said, sensing loss.

The troll held up his son's golden necklace. "You deserve this," he said softly.

I looked at the Golden Gloves necklace clutched in his old hand. The diamond in it sparkled. His troll eyes were, somehow, different—softer, gentler. Was he offering them to me?

"No," I said. "They're his. Americo deserves them."

"Yes," he said, nodding his head, "he does. You *both* do."

"Americo fought smart. They're his," I said.

"I'm proud—he beat the tiger. You was the best." Tears welled in Mr. Valero's eyes. He bowed his head.

"Thanks," I said, awkwardly.

"*Gracias, chico.*"

Tom, Mudbone and I walked down Thirty-first Street to the car. The bandage over Mudbone's left eye attracted quizzical glances from passers-by.

"It should never have been stopped," said Tom disgustedly.

"S'all right," said Mudbone.

"You was winnin'."

"Dat's life," said Mudbone, smiling.

"The bad thing about life," said Tom, scratching his gimped eye, is that it's very real."

As we crossed Ninth, a couple of things still bugged me.

"Tom?" I said.

"What you want?"

"What's in the bottle?"

Tom's one eye looked over at me. "You really want to know, don't you?"

"Yes."

"You got a real *problem,*" he said, chuckling, "with that bottle, don't you?"

"Yeah, sort of, I do."

"Well, my bottle," he chuckled, "ain't a problem to solve, it's a mystery to experience." He winked.

I was wasting my breath, I knew it. He would never tell me, so I stopped asking. Screw it.

We walked down the street. We were mute, except for Mudbone. Mudbone hummed a song.

"Mudbone?" I said.

"Huh?"

"What did the guys in the gym say about me?"

He shook his head. "Nothin'."

"C'mon."

"Probably ain't true anyhows."

"What did they say?" I repeated.

Mudbone laughed nervously. "They be sayin' that you once lived in, ya know . . ."

"In what?"

"A nuthouse . . . a mental institution."

I smiled. I thought of living with the Ceffones—trapped. Then I thought about graduating high school and the possibility of leaving that "mental institution" for college in a few months. "Not anymore," I said.

Mudbone eyed me.

As we walked down Thirty-first, I thought about my mother and my stepfather. I didn't like them, but that wouldn't matter much if I didn't live with them. They could live their life and I could live mine. Besides, I wanted to be through with hating; it didn't do me any good anymore. It was unnecessary. *Hating was poison.*

"I ever tell you my father was a songwriter?" I asked, suddenly—proudly.

"No," said Mudbone.

"He once had his song sung on 'The Tonight Show'."

"Yeah?"

"The Little Boy." I sang the ending:

> There came a time we said good-bye
> We've been apart since then.
> And no one knows as well as I
> He won't be back again.
> And though I search around the world,
> Until eternity,
> I'll never find that little boy,
> The boy I used to be.

"You *is* crazy, boy!" said Mudbone, laughing.

"Maybe," I said. But I knew I wasn't. For the first time in
years, my flesh didn't feel like a soft cage. I felt free.

I had hatched.

I fingered my necklace proudly. If I could survive the New
York Golden Gloves, I could survive anything. Nothing else
could frighten me for my entire life.

I had swallowed the toad!

retain 2 dot
5/15

fic
2 wk
new

°下乙

WOOD   COP.1
  TO SWALLOW A TOAD